USA TODAY BESTSELLING AUTHOR
NANCY WARREN

A CREAM
OF PASSION

THE GREAT WITCHES BAKING SHOW
BOOK 7

A Cream of Passion, The Great Witches Baking Show, book 7

ISBN: ebook 978-1-990210-11-2

ISBN: print 978-1-990210-10-5

Cover Design by Lou Harper of Cover Affairs

Ambleside Publishing

INTRODUCTION

Tempers are fraying and the cream is melting as summer temperatures hit the competition tent at Broomewode in the UK just in time for patisserie week. With only four contestants left, the pressure is mounting in the race to be chosen the best amateur baker in the UK. Poppy's working hard to find out who her parents were and what happened to them even as she's trying to become a more accomplished witch, so she definitely doesn't have time for romance. Then someone dies and it looks like a crime of passion. Can she unmask a killer before she's the one who gets creamed?

If you haven't met Rafe Crosyer yet, he's the gorgeous, sexy vampire in *The Vampire Knitting Club* series. You can get his origin story free when you join Nancy's no-spam newsletter at NancyWarrenAuthor.com.

Come join Nancy in her private Facebook group where we talk about books, knitting, pets and life.
www.facebook.com/groups/NancyWarrenKnitwits

A CREAM OF PASSION

"I'm going to miss having you in the tent, Poppy," Florence said. "But at least you're still here at Broomewode."

"Happily," I replied.

It was Friday afternoon, and I was back in Broomewode Village, but instead of trying to fight an onslaught of nerves ahead of a weekend of filming, I was here as a bona fide member of the community. I was a professional baker.

I'd been training with Sol, Broomewode Inn's head chef, all week, and tomorrow I'd be flying solo in my shiny new role as the inn's pastry chef. Florence had caught the train from London a day early, and we'd had lunch together at a little tea and sandwich shop after I finished my morning shift. Needless to say, with Florence around, the afternoon was about excess. We indulged in an enormous plate of finger sandwiches—soft white bread with the crusts removed and a dizzying array of fillings: egg and cress, chicken salad, cucumber and cream cheese, smoked ham and English mustard. A pretty ceramic bowl filled with salted potato chips (or crisps, as Florence kept correcting me) provided a satisfying crunch, and we drank pot after pot of steaming hot English Breakfast tea. Florence regaled me with stories of her three flatmates, all drama students and aspiring actors like her. I cracked up as she described squabbles over who was using the bathroom for too long or who had left dirty dishes in the sink again. The real drama of the week had involved two flatmates auditioning for the same role in a small theater's production of Chekhov's *Three Sisters*. "You should have heard them trying to rehearse the same lines louder than each other in their bedrooms," Florence said. "I had to turn up the radio to drown out their wailing. *I don't know why I'm so happy,*" she mimicked, placing her palm to her forehead. "*What beautiful thoughts I had, what thoughts!*"

Florence really cracked me up, and I expressed my sympathies for her plight, of course, but truthfully, I couldn't imagine sharing my little cottage with anyone. I'd been living alone for the past four years, and it was bliss. Gina, my best friend, was a short drive away and had her own set of keys to let herself in. I loved Gina to the moon and back, but would I want to live with her? No way. How could I ever share a bathroom with that girl? Hair and beauty were her trade, and she practiced what she preached. I'd never be able to shower, let alone blow-dry my hair! I'd become so accustomed to guarding myself constantly from accidentally interacting with ghosts when I was in public that I enjoyed being able to relax completely when I was home alone. Not completely alone, of course, because I had Mildred, my kitchen ghost, constantly prattling on, plus Gateau, my familiar, who had her ways of communicating, but neither of them took up counter space in the bathroom or hogged the shower.

Even when I left Mildred behind, I'd arrive in Broomewode to find Gerry, a recent and not very happy ghost waiting to show me his latest tricks.

Walking arm in arm with Florence through the village streets, I'd never felt so lucky. I had a new job, great friends in the village, and I was back on the trail to find out more about my birth parents. After Trim, a reporter for the *Broomewode News,* had put me in touch with Mavis (an inside editor at the same paper), I'd had my first proper lead about my birth mom in ages. I'd actually gone to the newspaper to find out my dad's name by scouring the old obituaries, but after having no luck, Mavis had recognized the name Valerie —she was an old school friend of her daughter, Joanna. I'd been elated, of course, and had scribbled down Joanna's details with glee. I fired off an email to her as soon as I got a moment alone. She was a solicitor, dealing with property, or so the website told me. So I wrote a short but hopefully compelling email explaining that I had some questions about a property in Broomewode Village. I figured that would be the quickest way to get Joanna's attention. I could explain more when I got her on the phone. I got a reply in seconds, but sadly it was an out-of-office. She was away on business and would be back at work Friday afternoon. Which meant I could call her as soon as Florence and I parted ways. I was beyond excited to finally speak to someone who had known my mom.

It had rained during the week, a light, refreshing drizzle, and the flowers and plants thrived from the hearty drink and were more abundant and dazzling than ever. The sun had returned from its brief vacation and was back with a vengeance, ready to outshine itself for the weekend.

"Pops, you're doing that thing again. The one where you look all dreamy and stop listening."

I apologized and told Florence that all my baking secrets were hers now that we were no longer in head-to-head competition. It was why I was steering her around the village streets in the direction of my most secret and treasured baking weapon: Broomewode Farm.

"I've always wanted to visit the farm," Florence cooed. "But you were always dashing off on some mission or another. Susan seems very charming, and I think her special friend Reginald is quite the silver fox."

Ha, trust Florence to have spotted Reg's finer qualities. Did that girl ever learn?

"Well, her eggs will blow your mind," I said, merrily skipping over the more personal comments. "She calls them her happy eggs, as her hens are so content, roaming outdoors eating organic treats. The yolks are the most perfect shade of orange you'll ever see. They make the most incredible sponge."

"Good for dessert week?" Florence said, her big eyes widening.

I'd almost forgotten that this week was dessert week on *The Great British Baking Contest*. I hadn't allowed my imagination to travel any further than each week I'd managed to get through.

"Of course!" I replied. "I can't believe we haven't discussed your recipes yet. Tell me everything."

Florence flicked her perfect chestnut curls over her shoulders and took a deep breath.

"The signature bake is cheesecake, which is my favorite dessert of all time, except for maybe sticky toffee pudding or rhubarb crumble. Oh, who am I kidding? I love *all* desserts."

She went on to excitedly tell me all about her own secret weapon—Amalfi lemons—as I continued to gently steer her along the pretty residential streets, away from the shops around the village green. It seemed like everyone who lived in Broomewode was house proud, each front garden full to the brim with flowers in bloom, lush green grass neatly trimmed. The windows gleamed, and the pastel hues of each home were as cute as candies.

Moms were out walking with their strollers, no doubt heading to the little park near the green where the kids could play on swings and exhausted parents could gossip over take-away lattes from the coffee shop opposite. It was an idyllic scene, innocent and warm, and I hugged myself tightly, still in disbelief at how I'd managed to land on my feet after being eliminated during bread week. Felled by bread! I still couldn't believe it.

However, as Florence chatted about the show, I only felt relief that I no longer had to compete. I didn't have enough ambition to make it all the way to the show's finale. I knew that perfectly well. But even still—I thought I'd feel a smidgen of jealousy this week at how everyone would continue having fun without me.

"I only hope that it has enough zing to wow Jonathon. He's definitely my toughest critic."

I nodded. "Jonathon does tend to be harder on everyone than Elspeth, but you might be surprised to find he's a pussycat underneath that tough exterior."

Florence abruptly stopped in her tracks. "Come on, Poppy. What do you know that I don't?"

I grinned and shook my head. Florence would be shocked if she discovered that both judges, the famous Jonathon Pine and the even more famous Elspeth Peach, were witches. Like me. I'd pay good money to see Florence's expression if I ever spilled those very secret beans. But these were secrets I'd have to take to my grave. Witches' honor and all that. I told Florence there was no gossip to spill—just my intuition told me that Jonathon's brutal comments were all for the camera.

"Besides," I said, "you're about to gain access to my biggest baking secret."

As we turned onto the path to Broomewode Farm, a familiar sound filled my ears.

"What's that weird panting?" Florence asked, confused.

I laughed. "Just give it a second." And then there he was: Sly! Slobbering all over his favorite ball as usual.

"Aren't you adorable," Florence cooed, bending down to stroke Sly's soft black and white fur. He jumped up, excited by the attention, leaving mucky paw marks on Florence's pristine cropped black trousers. To my surprise, she laughed off the mud, casually brushing it away from the expensive fabric. "I've seen this one before. He's got a real personality."

Oh, she didn't know the half of it. Sly was my sister witch Susan's familiar but also a truly goofy border collie. "My family are big on dogs," she said whimsically. "We kept Afghan hounds when I was young."

Sly didn't waste a second putting Florence to work and nudged his ball towards her feet.

"Careful," I warned. "Once you start with that ball, he'll never let you stop."

"Then we'll just have to spend all day being best friends, won't we, sweet thing?" Florence said, throwing the ball.

Sly raced after the ball, and we continued. As we rounded a corner, Susan's huge barn came into view, and then the curved roof and the local Somerset stone of the farmhouse. I heard the now familiar shift from crunch to silence as the path switched out wood chips for stone and the flowerbeds changed to laurel hedging and bright springy fern. Susan's garden was spilling over with luscious green herbs. Sly bounded ahead, barking happily as he chased after the ball.

Hearing Sly bark, Susan emerged from the farmhouse, her short hair swept back in a peach headscarf and a huge ball of indigo yarn in her hands. "Poppy and Florence. Lovely to see you," she said in her deep voice. Susan held up the yarn. "What do you think?" she asked. "I've been experimenting with different natural dyes, and I think this is the best yet. I thought it could be fun to sell alongside our honey and other produce at the market."

"Gorgeous," Florence said, stepping closer to inspect the wool. "I'd love a sweater in this color. It would make a very chic winter scarf, too."

Susan chuckled. "This one can come over anytime," she said to me. "Come inside. Let's get you some tea and then I'll fetch Florence some of my very special happy eggs." At Florence's expression of surprise, Susan said, "That is why you're here, isn't it?"

"Yes, but how clever of you to guess," Florence said.

"Sol asked for another four dozen for the kitchen," I piped up, suddenly remembering my new boss's request.

"And how's it going, working for Sol? He certainly has a fiery streak in him."

I laughed. "Sol might look a little brutish, and he's definitely good at barking orders, but inside he's a sweet puppy dog—just like Sly here." I petted Susan's familiar. "Sol just cares a lot about what he does. It makes him sound more intense than he is."

"I do like a man with passion," Florence said as Susan led us into her big kitchen.

I shot her a hard look.

"But after last week," she said hurriedly, "I've sworn off men forever."

Susan shook her head as she filled the kettle. "Nasty business. Who knew that the charming Darius was such a rotter?"

Sly barked. Did he sense danger at the mere mention of Darius's name?

Florence blushed. "Certainly not me," she said meekly.

I'd never seen Florence bashful before, but she had reason after her fling with Darius, the charismatic Greek barman at Broomewode Inn, had ended in complete disaster and nearly cost her life.

We chatted about the show and how nervous Florence was. Conversation usually revolved around Florence when she was present. Susan brewed a pot of tea, filling the kitchen with the fragrance.

"Poppy?" Susan said, smiling at me gently. "Here's your tea." She passed me a mug. I took a sip. It was her own mixture. I tasted chamomile, lavender, rosehip, and mint. There were other subtle flavors I couldn't identify. I added a dollop of honey from her happy bees, and when I sipped again, I was instantly soothed.

"I heard they've been interviewing for Darius's replacement," Susan said.

I nodded. "A new girl starts tonight. Eve was pleased. She's young and keen, but this is her first job, I think."

Susan smiled a little whimsically and rubbed her right temple. I waited for her to tell us what her first job had been, but she stayed silent, perhaps enjoying the nostalgia.

"I've never really had a job-job," Florence said, "you know, like a shopgirl or sweeping up hair in the hairdressers. My mum had me child-modeling from the age of two. I was very sweet as a kid, I have to say. My mum would brush my hair up into a big pineapple on top of my head."

I laughed. *Of course* Florence had been a child model.

"I guess that's where my love of being in front of the cameras came from," she continued.

"You're a natural, from what I hear," Susan said. "I prefer to avoid the limelight, myself. Happier pottering away behind the scenes. Speaking of which—why don't you come and visit the chickens with me? You can pick your own happy eggs."

Florence beamed, and the three of us finished up our tea and headed outside. Sly bounded ahead, no doubt excited to terrorize the chickens with his herding skills, but Susan called him back. "Sly. Guard the house."

Sly bowed his head a little but obeyed the command, turning round and rushing back to the kitchen's side door.

"Aww," Florence said.

"Save your sympathies for another scamp." Susan laughed. "Sly knows he can't play with the chickens. They don't take kindly to being herded."

"I'm certain I'll make a winning cheesecake with a few of your happy eggs."

Florence linked her arm through Susan's and then mine, and like the three musketeers of baking, we went to see what the happy chickens had gifted us.

~

WALKING BACK to the inn with a brimming basket, Florence chatted away about her plans for the weekend. It was so much nicer to be swept along in her enthusiasm for the show rather than competing in it myself. The afternoon sun provided a delicious warmth, and I felt lucky the next chapter of my life was here in the village where I was sure my parents had met. One more hour and I'd call Joanna. My heart raced at the thought.

We stepped onto the path leading back to the inn when a sudden cool breeze washed over me, and with it came the sound of a man singing. It was so unexpected and sounded like the Three Tenors CD my dad used to play way too loud. We stopped walking. I tilted my head and listened.

"Where on earth is it coming from?" I asked. The voice grew louder, more forceful.

"It's so beautiful!" Florence said. Her expression became dreamy and distant. She closed her eyes and smiled. "'Nessun Dorma.' Pavarotti himself sang that at the Turin Olympics opening ceremonies."

"No way!" I said. "That's so cool. Is he singing in Italian?"

Florence nodded, eyes still closed. "It translates into 'Let No One Sleep.'" I thought no one would be able to sleep if this singer took it upon himself to break into song at bedtime.

The voice grew stronger, and suddenly a man burst out onto the path in front of us and the singing stopped. He blushed, obviously startled by his unintended audience. I recognized him as Luca, the owner of the village deli, where Florence ordered in her Italian ingredients.

Immediately, Florence burst into a flurry of excited Italian. The man's blush deepened.

I didn't have to understand Italian to be certain Florence was gushing about his wonderful singing.

Luca laughed, answering in English. "You should hear me in the shower. More drama than all the Italian arias strung together."

As he chuckled, he shifted a bulging tote bag from one shoulder to the other. He was wearing a long-sleeved linen shirt like hikers wear, probably to keep bugs and brambles from biting him. Luca noticed our bags. Along with eggs and honey, Susan had given us both tall fronds of rhubarb. I had plans to make mine into breakfast pastries, while Florence had wondered if she might incorporate the fruit into one of her desserts.

"I, too, have been foraging," he told us. Then he tapped the side of his nose and closed one eye as though he were a spy who'd been behind enemy lines.

I turned to Florence, whose eyes were shining. She loved to be in on any kind of local knowledge—especially if it involved ingredients. "What is it?"

I wasn't beyond a few local tips myself, so I listened eagerly.

He lowered his voice to a whisper even though there wasn't a single human being in sight. "First, you must swear to secrecy," he said mystically, a sly smile playing at the corners of his mouth.

Florence and I swore. I could see that she was enjoying the buildup.

After pausing for a moment, Luca decided we could be trusted. "I found a secret patch of early chanterelle mushrooms beside a field of wild garlic." He made a murmur of pleasure. "Together they will taste sublime."

"Oooh," Florence exhaled. "I love chanterelles."

Luca agreed. "Chanterelles and wild garlic are a match made in heaven. And heaven shouldn't be kept waiting. I'm going to create a wonderful fresh pasta dinner with them tonight."

"Oh, how wonderful." Florence sighed.

I could feel myself begin to salivate. Fresh pasta was such a treat. Luca chuckled and asked if we'd like to join him. "There's plenty to go around," he said, "and ingredients like these need to be shared."

"We'd love to," Florence blurted out, assuming (quite rightly) that I didn't have any plans.

I laughed.

"Are you sure you young ladies don't have other plans for a Friday night?"

Florence shook her head. "Nothing more important than tasting fresh produce. Plus, I suddenly have an idea for chanterelles in an upcoming bake."

"You always have wonderful ideas."

"Oh, and you got my email? About the vanilla pods and Italian almond paste? I need it this weekend."

"Of course. I'll bring them home from the shop and you can pick them up this evening."

I nodded, never one to turn down a fabulous meal. He invited us to arrive at seven-thirty, and we thanked him. I tried not to think about how long an Italian dinner could last and how early I had to be at work in the morning.

"What a treat," she said as the three of us continued down the path together. "I'll feel like I'm back home in Italy."

CHAPTER 2

*A*fter saying goodbye to Florence, I walked to the rose garden to find the bench where I'd once sat with Elspeth Peach when she first explained that I was a witch, like her. I didn't know why I was drawn there. Perhaps it was drawing *me* to *it*. We were now officially at the beginning of summer, and the air was full of floral perfume and the buzz of hardworking bees. It was a serene, quiet place, despite being within view of the white calico baking tent where technicians were as busy as my local bees getting everything ready for filming tomorrow. This felt like the right place to sit and make the phone call to Joanna.

I'd been waiting for this all week, but now that the time had come, I was suddenly nervous. I closed my eyes and took a deep breath. Why was I so worried? Maybe facing my past was going to be harder than I'd anticipated. I mean, my birth mother had left me in an apple box outside a bakery when I was probably only a few hours old. It was difficult not to feel outrage and resentment on behalf of that helpless infant.

Still, I'd come this far and couldn't let nerves get the

better of me now. I was on the cusp of learning the truth about my parents, something I'd wanted for as long as I could remember. Okay, Valerie wasn't going to be in line for mother of the year, but we were bonded by blood. Besides, my witch powers had come from somewhere. Had she been a witch too?

I settled myself on the oak bench, letting my fingertips feel the ancient grooves that rippled through the wood. I hadn't noticed before that the bench arms were curved, ornate cast iron that curled gracefully. How I'd love to know how many people had sat here before me. Couples having heart-to-hearts, crying on a best friend's shoulder, giggling on the phone to their sister or perhaps just sitting quietly, reading a book with their face warmed by the sun. "You probably know all the village secrets," I whispered, "the good, the bad, the ugly. If only I could ask you about my mom and dad. I'd bet a pretty pound that you'd know the answer."

I closed my eyes and recalled the words Elspeth had said to me as the truth about my witchy powers became clear. *It is a great privilege and an honor to be a witch, Poppy. You will have come from a great line of witches in your family. It is passed down through the maternal side. No wonder you feel such a strong urge to find your mother."*

I opened my eyes again and touched the amethyst necklace that lay flat against my blue T-shirt. Working in the kitchen earlier meant that I hadn't worn Eve's amulet bracelet —it dangled down and got in the way as I was mixing—but now I felt naked without it. Already I was so used to feeling the energy of the great Team Poppy. But strangely I could sense Eve's warm vibes around me, protecting me, even though she was on the other side of the grounds. "I'm getting closer, Mom," I whispered, half talking to an image in my head, half talking to the bench. "I promise to keep an open mind."

I took out my phone and found the number of Joanna's office from my saved contacts. Deep down, I knew I should wait for her to reply to my email. I'd left my number and asked her to call me as soon as she was back in the office. I had no reason to think she'd delay, but I couldn't stand waiting any longer. It was time for answers, and I was ready to demand them.

With trembling hands, I hit the saved number to Joanna's office in Bristol.

The phone rang for what seemed an unreasonable amount of time. With each new ring, my heart moved another inch towards my throat. "Come on, Joanna, come on," I whispered into the phone.

I was about to hang up when the phone clicked and a breathless voice said, "Hello? Mercantile Solicitors."

I realized I'd been holding my breath and let it exhale. Was that Joanna herself answering? Part of my search was finally going to plan. About time.

"Oh, hello, is this Joanna? My name is Poppy Wilkinson. I sent you an email. I'm looking for some information."

The woman continued to catch her breath for a moment before replying. "Yes, this is she. Sorry, I just ran to the phone. I've been at a conference this week, and I only just walked through the door."

Now that her breathing was regulating, I could hear that Joanna had a honeyed, cultured voice—calm and measured even though I'd caught her off-guard. I had a sudden picture of her kicking away a pair of heeled navy pumps as she spoke and settling into a brown leather office chair, smoothing down a sensible pencil skirt and unbuttoning the top of a pristinely ironed shirt. Was it one of my visions or simply my imagination acting up? I apologized again.

And then, in a very British exchange, Joanna said she was sorry too—she'd yet to tackle the mountain that was her inbox. "A few days away and I come back to an avalanche, I'm afraid. It'll take me all weekend to work my way through. Was it an urgent query?"

I said I understood, although in truth most of the emails I received these days were from my mom and dad who'd retired in France, a work rota from Sol, and a surprisingly frequent newsletter from a hardware store where I'd once bought pliers—hmm, I should really remember to unsubscribe.

"Well, it's probably best I caught you on the phone," I said, feeling my mouth dry up. It was now or never.

I suspected she'd pulled a pad of paper and pen toward herself. "How can I help you?"

Okay, deep breath, Pops. You've got this.

I gave Joanna my well-rehearsed "I'm looking for my cousin" story, the one I'd practiced with Katie Donegal, Trim Trimble, and then Joanna's mother, Mavis, at the local paper. I explained that I was now working at Broomewode Inn and had heard that a distant male cousin might have lived in the area, perhaps even worked at the same inn. (I had to admit, I was kind of enjoying embellishing the story. And the more detail, the more convincing the lie, right?)

"I visited Broomewode's newspaper office and met your mom," I said.

She didn't speak or interrupt, and I wondered if I was

coming across a little strange. Who was in such a hurry to track down a distant cousin? "She was trying to help me," I continued hurriedly, "but as I don't have his name, it proved impossible. All I had to go on was the name of a girl he might have dated."

There was a pause, and I could almost hear Joanna's eyes rolling. "Okaaaay," she said hesitantly and with a lick of impatience. "I'm still not sure how I can help here. Did he own a house in the village?"

"Maybe," I said. "Your mom told me that you might be able to shed some light on the matter, as you went to school with a girl he was dating." I paused, suddenly terrified I was about to be told something awful. Where had this feeling of dread come from? *Get it together, Pops!* "Her name was Valerie. Do you remember her?"

The line went silent. Had she hung up on me? Surely not! And then Joanna spoke in a much quieter voice than before. "Valerie. My goodness, that's a long time ago. How old are you?"

"I'm sorry?"

Joanna said, "It's just that I have a daughter, and you sound about her age."

Huh. Was that supposed to make things less weird?

"I'm twenty-five," I said finally, figuring there was no harm in telling the truth about my age.

"Ah, a little older than my girl," Joanna said. "Look, I'm happy to answer any questions I can about Valerie's love life, but I'm afraid my school days are woefully very far behind me. I need a few days to get through my workload, and then I'll see if I can fish out my photograph albums from that era and see if it jogs my memory. I'm actually visiting my mother next Friday, so I'll be in Broomewode. Shall we meet then? Perhaps at the tea shop for some coffee?"

My heart soared. Joanna was willing to talk face-to-face? Despite having to wait another week for answers, a real-life meeting was worth it. I agreed enthusiastically, and Joanna said she'd send a text next week to confirm times.

"I do really have to get going now, I'm afraid," Joanna said. "Much to do."

I thanked her profusely for her time. "I know how precious it is," I said. "Looking forward to seeing you next week."

With a quick "till then," Joanna hung up, and I sat staring at my cell phone, feeling a little bamboozled. The call hadn't gone as I'd planned but possibly better than I'd dared to hope. She remembered Valerie. Then I thought about that strange question about my age. Had she known Valerie when she got pregnant? Could she possibly suspect my mission was a joint one, to find my father and my mother?

"Hmm," I said to the now-black screen of my phone. Was Joanna buying time to fob me off, or did she really need to filter her inbox and get out the old photo albums before speaking to me properly? Either way, now I had no choice but to wait. Besides, if she *was* going through old photos, she'd no doubt bring some when she visited next week. Maybe that would mean I could get another glimpse of my mom, even younger than the photo I had of her at the Broomewode Hall garden party. I smiled to myself. Had my mom been a cool teenager, or pimpled and kind of rumpled like I was growing up? I felt my smile get even wider. I loved the idea of seeing my mom as a child.

But no more musing. I had to get back to the inn and

make sure that Sol gave me another split shift next Friday. Nothing could get in the way of me meeting with Joanna— not even a brand-new job. As I began to walk back, my heart sank as I remembered that I'd promised Florence to accompany her to Luca's for dinner. All I wanted was to drive home, snuggle with my cat Gateau, check in on Mildred the kitchen ghost, and relax in front of the TV with a super simple dinner.

However, being invited to eat freshly foraged chanterelles cooked by an Italian who loved to cook, I would soon get over myself.

CHAPTER 3

*B*ack at the inn, everything looked the same as it had for the last six weekends, except I had to remind myself that it wasn't. Things were completely different now. This was my place of work, not relaxation after being on TV in a baking competition. No more long dinners with the other contestants, no more being a minor celebrity. I was paid to work. The pub was busy, and a party atmosphere was building as the afternoon slipped into Friday evening and the village began to relax. Tables were already crowded with the early dinner crowd, those catching up with friends and family over a bottle of chilled white or rich, relaxing red. As usual, Eve had provided the homey touches the inn was famed for, and accompanying the church candles flickering along the windowsills and tables, small posies of iris and delphiniums were arranged in bud vases. Their bright blues and pinks brought the outside in. Meanwhile, delicious smells drifted out from the kitchen. It really was a glorious place to end the week.

And then I saw that the remaining *Great British Baking*

Contest contestants were gathered around our usual table. I meant their usual table (it would probably take a while to get used to not counting myself as part of the baking crew). In previous weeks, the group had been sprawling, taking up the spare chairs and spilling into the room. Now they'd well and truly shrunk and used less than half the table they'd once dominated. With only Gaurav, Maggie, Hamish, and Florence left, the bakers must have been consumed by nerves. But if Florence was worried, she didn't show it. Instead, she waved at me manically across the room like we hadn't just seen each other, leapt from her seat and, grabbing me by the hand, led me over to where they sat. She pulled out a chair in a very chivalrous fashion.

"Poppy!" Hamish greeted me, beaming. "So glad you're here today. How has your week been? Is the new job fun? What have you been baking? We're all dying to know. And to order later! I didn't get to try enough of your creations in the tent."

I laughed at the onslaught of questions and answered them one by one. "Great; super fun but hard work; lots of pastries and chocolate cake."

"And is Sol a tough boss?" Gaurav asked.

I opened my mouth to reply, but Florence took it upon herself to answer for me. "Poppy says Sol is a pussycat at heart, but I don't believe her for a second. She's putting on a brave face—any actress would be able to spot it a mile off."

I giggled, protesting. Why did no one believe me when I said Sol was a softie underneath his brawler's body covered with tattoos?

"Anyway," I said, "I don't want to talk about work—I want

to catch up on the goss. Who is making what for dessert week? Spill the cocoa beans."

Maggie leaned in, her eyes widening. "I'm trying my hand at something very different this weekend. No more traditional recipes—this time I'm pulling something very special out of the proverbial icing bag."

The rest of the group fell silent. Maggie was the sweet grandmother of the group. Everyone expected her to turn out traditional fare, and so far she had, and it was such fabulous quality that she'd made it to the final four. She seemed sharper, more alert than I'd ever noticed before. Was this Maggie's competitive genes kicking into gear? She was kitted out in her usual uniform of twin set and slacks, but today the colors were more muted in shades of taupe, devoid of frills or applique, and there was a simple gold pendant at her neck in place of her usual string of pearls. Maggie pushed her gold-rimmed spectacles to the end of her nose and looked at each of us in turn. "It's a black forest meringue cake."

"Oooh," Florence said. "I adore a black forest gateau."

I "mmm-ed" my agreement.

"The meringue takes it to a whole new level," Maggie continued. "Crunchy and soft at the same time. The trick is soaking morello cherries in good quality brandy. I've been practicing all week."

"That's the stuff," Hamish said, licking his lips. But he also looked worried. Gaurav, too—a slight crease in his forehead deepened. Surely they weren't feeling threatened by Maggie's confession. It wasn't *that* radical. But there was a palpable tension in the air. Maybe it had always been there and I'd been too consumed by the competition and my own nervous energy to notice it before. For the remaining bakers, perhaps it was the realization that winning was now actually within sight, but so was losing. It had to feel scary. I couldn't imagine that any of the bakers had envisaged themselves at the finish line—except for Florence, of course. She was the only one who appeared confident and in control. But since she'd spent so long training to be an actress, perhaps there was a lot more going on under the surface than she showed.

I tuned back in to the excited chatter.

"Chocolate panna cotta," Florence was saying, "sitting on top of a light as a cloud savarin sponge, and the whole thing finished off with butterscotch popcorn bites for crunch."

"Ooh, that's good," Gaurav said softly. "So many textures and complementary flavors. But how are you going to make the panna cotta? When I do one at home, it has to set for at least six hours. Aren't you worried? What if the gelatin doesn't dissolve properly?"

The others nodded. I'd never made panna cotta myself, but it was definitely something I enjoyed when it was served to me. It would never have occurred to me to make a chocolate version of the creamy, vanilla dessert.

Florence wasn't ruffled in the slightest by Gaurav's question. She explained that she'd been practicing with a blast chiller in a nearby friend's restaurant. The panna cotta would set if she made it first, superfast, and got it straight into the chiller.

"I think I work best under pressure," Florence added, leaning over the table to top up her wine.

"Not me," Gaurav said quietly. "The nerves take over. When one of the judges calls out our starting time, it takes everything I've got to stop my legs from collapsing into jelly. And I imagine this weekend will feel worse than ever."

Maggie patted Gaurav's arm. "You have to stay positive, dearest. Everyone is under the same time constraints, suffering the same nerves. But the mind can triumph over the body's reaction."

I took a sip of wine and stayed quiet. It was weird: I both belonged and didn't belong in this conversation. I knew exactly what the group was feeling, but it was no longer my problem.

"I don't want this journey to end," Gaurav said.

There were murmurs of agreement from everyone else. I felt myself turning a little pink. Did no one realize that the journey had, in fact, ended for me? Like, very abruptly, very recently?

"Not the most tactful bunch, are they?" said a voice from behind.

I should have guessed my spirit-friend wouldn't have been able to resist a little eavesdropping on the eve of the quarterfinal of the show. I cocked my head to the left slightly and caught sight of Gerry's floating grin.

"I mean, talk about rubbing salt in the wound. Or maybe that should be sugar in the wound, huh?"

I tried to shrug surreptitiously.

"Come back and talk to me when there's no one around," Gerry said. "I've learned some new tricks."

I made a small nodding motion, wondering why he didn't seem able to move on. As for new tricks, he had nothing but time, poor dear. He had new tricks and only me to show off to.

"There's a twenty-five percent chance of being voted off of the show," Gaurav was saying.

"When you put it like that, it sounds so high," Florence said, finally looking worried.

"I'm not ready to leave," Hamish said. "It's like, the longer we stay, the harder it is to deal with the chance of being voted off."

But Maggie just waved her hands. "We have to stay bright and optimistic. None of these miserable talk of percentages."

"It's not pessimistic," Gaurav insisted. "It's facts. I deal with data every day. There's no arguing that if four of us are left and one will be sent home this weekend, then each of us has a twenty-five percent chance of leaving."

The group fell silent. I had no idea what to say. Should I tell them it's not so bad to be cast from the show? That, in fact, it could open up a world of new opportunities? That next exciting thing was around the corner if you kept your eyes open to it.

But luckily, I didn't have to expound any platitudes. Hamish took the cue to lighten the mood and began to describe his signature cheesecake recipe—a cookie dough cheesecake "mash-up."

"The idea came from babysitting my niece and nephew. I say babysitting—they're thirteen and fourteen and act like they're twenty-one sometimes but still not too old to want to lick the bowl. Anyway, I was at my sister's house last week and she wanted an hour's peace and quiet, so I took the kids into the kitchen and asked them to help me experiment. They both thought the best part of baking was eating raw cookie dough. And together we came up with the idea of a cheesecake with a chocolate chip cookie crust and little pearls of balls of cookie dough throughout the batter. Once it's baked, I slather the whole thing in a cookie-dough frosting and pieces of crisp chocolate chip cookies."

"Sounds like cookie dough heaven," I said, wanting to eat some right now. "And it's a great story with your family getting involved. So many people at home will be able to relate to that. I know I certainly can." Some of my happiest memories as a kid were helping my best friend Gina's dad at his bakery.

"Me too," Florence said. "I was always tearing off bits of raw cookie dough when my nona was baking and nibbling at them when she wasn't looking. I was a real scamp in the kitchen."

"Nothing changes." Hamish laughed.

Florence smiled good-naturedly. "Okay, I *am* a real scamp in the kitchen," she corrected. A wistful look came over her then. "It's the second time today I've had a palpable memory of Italy. I used to spend all the school holidays there as a kid, and now it's been over a year since I was with my extended family, sunning myself on a golden beach and living the dolce vita."

I smiled as Florence described her family's village, but a flash of envy crept in there, too. It must have been so nice growing up with so many family members around. My adoptive parents had done an amazing job of making sure I met as many of our family as possible. But they were scattered around the United States; some had emigrated to Australia— I even had some distant cousins in Nepal. And now my folks lived in the south of France. It must be nice for Florence to have everyone in one place. She was so good with words that I could actually see her busy household: a charming stone building with cool tiled floor, the kitchen at the back of the

26

house overlooking a pretty herb garden and a small pool carved from stone.

"And the scent of Amalfi lemons," Florence was saying. "There's nothing quite like it. I've got my whole spiel ready to talk to the cameras about my Amalfi lemon cheesecake."

Hamish clapped his hands together, "Och, I love it when you say your lines. For the life of me, I can never remember what I want to say."

Immediately, Florence snapped to attention, straightening her back and letting her chest sit forward a little. She pushed her long, thick hair over her shoulders so that it hung in beautiful waves and cleared her throat. "Well, Jonathon, my family are from the Amalfi Coast, so naturally I was raised on our delicious lemons. No ordinary citrus fruit, the Amalfi lemon has thick and wrinkled skin with an intense perfume and a sweet and juicy flesh. Don't tell anyone, but the secret to the taste and the special properties of the *sfusato amalfitano* is all down to the porous, naturally fertilized soil of the Amalfi. It's protected from the cold northern wind by the mountains but exposed to the sea breezes and strong sun. On the coast, we use the whole fruit in our cuisine: the juice, the flesh, the peel, and even the leaves."

Florence drew a deep breath and flashed her most winning, white-toothed smile. Everyone clapped bravo. Maybe this was where I'd gone wrong on the show—I hadn't gotten in touch with my inner diva enough. Just the thought even made me snort a little into my wineglass.

"I don't know about you all," Hamish said, "but that little speech really got my appetite going. Shall we have an early supper?"

Florence practically squealed. "Goodness, what's the time? Poppy and I have been invited out to dinner."

Hamish looked sternly at me. "Shouldn't you be resting up? I hear you start work very early so we have fresh breads and pastries for our breakfast."

I laughed and promised I'd make sure there were plenty of freshly baked delicacies for tomorrow's breakfast. I explained we were having a friendly supper with a local business owner. I was going to tell them about meeting Luca and his secret stash of chanterelles, but Florence sent me a quick frown. Right. She wanted to keep that secret in case she needed fresh chanterelles herself.

Florence turned and took me by the hand. "Now let's get you upstairs and freshened up. You can't be turning up to dinner in a flour-covered T-shirt."

I looked down. For the first time, I noticed the puffs of white flour on the side of my top and a small stain where I'd spilled sugar syrup. Great. I loved how she waited till now to tell me. Now that I was staff and not on the baking show, I didn't get a nice room at the inn. I had an assigned locker for keeping my belongings and a change of clothes. I grabbed a clean outfit and came back to the dining room where Florence was waiting. I'd change in her room.

I wished the others a lovely dinner and followed Florence upstairs. I was tired, and Hamish was right—I did have another early morning to look forward to. As if she'd read my mind, Florence suddenly said, "You'll feel better once you've changed, Pops. Besides, think of the glorious wild garlic pesto and the fresh chanterelles."

She had me there. I'd pretty much do anything for a beautiful dinner I didn't have to cook.

CHAPTER 4

*F*lorence strode straight up to Luca's front door and pressed the buzzer three times. It burst into a surprisingly loud *zzt, zzt, zzt.* I hung back, hovering a little way from the shop. Luca lived above the deli, which must have been very convenient for work, but there was something strange about approaching the shop and asking to come in when the silver shutters were down. I knew that behind the window lay a delightful display of taralli biscuits, dried pasta, canned butter beans, and artichokes. Shelves burst with baking goods and produce that would brighten any pantry. But the whole street felt abandoned, silent, and an unfamiliar sense of disquiet in my own body was growing by the moment.

Why was I feeling so nervous? It wasn't like I wasn't good at talking to people, and I was constantly leaping headfirst into new, and often precarious, situations. I was the girl who'd talked her way into the grand Broomewode Hall on more than one occasion despite the snooty earl and countess trying to keep me out. Maybe it was my clothes. I tugged at the pastel shirt Florence had insisted that I borrow this evening. I tried to laugh off her suggestion that she do my makeup, but Florence being Florence had worn me down, and I sat like a patient doll while she swiftly did my eyes and hair. To be fair to my beautiful friend, the shirt was gorgeous —a pale pink linen with voluptuous sleeves that billowed in the breeze. And tucking it into my indigo jeans was, to her credit, a quick way to smarten my look and give the illusion of a waist I didn't really own. But, pretty as it was, I simply didn't feel myself. It was too fussy to fit my style, and the vivid pink lipstick she paired it with was perfect but again, too daring, too much of a statement, for me to feel truly comfortable. It was all adding up to an uncomfortable sensation of not being right in my own skin.

Florence turned round. "What you are doing all the way over there, silly goose?" she chided. She motioned me over. "He's taking forever to come down the stairs." She checked her watch. "We're a couple of minutes early, which is like a miracle for me. I think it's your good influence, Pops. Besides, I'm hungry."

"Maybe he's got a few pots and pans on the go," I suggested, "and he'll be down when they're under control?" I smiled weakly, wishing that I was back in my cozy cottage in Norton St. Philip. I was missing Gateau, who no doubt was curled up on her favorite armchair while Mildred, my kitchen ghost, wafted about the place waiting for me to come back so she could complain about how long I'd been gone. But Florence was such a compelling force, it was easy to get swept up in her energy and enthusiasm—and, as it turned out, her enormous wardrobe of clothes that she hauled from London every weekend.

"I'll try again," Florence said after a few moments passed. She buzzed and we waited, Florence chatting about wild garlic, but I couldn't focus on the words. My brain was distracted, like it couldn't streamline its own thoughts.

"Are you cold?" I asked, suddenly shivering and cutting Florence off mid-sentence. "I feel like there's a chill in the air."

Florence shook her head, and her hair swung like a shampoo commercial. She was wearing a black two-piece, a simple pencil skirt and loose sleeveless tunic, a chunky silver chain at her neck and matching bracelet at her wrist. It was the epitome of understated European style.

I shivered again. "Really? Not even your arms?"

"It's pretty warm out, Poppy." She took a quick step back. "Could you be coming down with something?"

"Just chilly, I think. What's going on with Luca? We've been out here ages. Do you think he's forgotten?"

"How could he forget a dinner date with us?"

The shuttered deli really did feel eerie, like something sinister was lurking behind its locked exterior. Was my imagination being overactive?

"I dunno. Something doesn't feel right."

Florence insisted that Luca simply couldn't hear us and pressed the buzzer for a third time, this time letting her finger linger, drawing out the sharp sounds until they merged into one long, jarring note. The silence after it finished was even more noticeable. But then, listening more carefully, the sound of opera reached us. It was faint, almost imperceptible, but I could just make out a strong tenor voice.

"Do you hear that?" I asked. Why hadn't we noticed before?

Florence nodded. "It must be drowning out the buzzer." She paused, lost in thought. "I'd ring the shop phone, but I doubt he'll hear that either. Perhaps there's a resident's entrance round the back?"

The last thing I wanted to do was to go snooping around Luca's property, but Florence wouldn't shift. "We can't just *leave,* he's invited us to dinner. We're expected."

Florence made her way round the side of the store to a little alleyway that served as a thoroughfare to the road behind. I followed. Florence was very adept at making me feel like her younger, more inhibited sister. The cold in me intensified. Every hair on my arms stood to attention.

I realized we were standing right by a back door that was swinging on its hinges. "See," Florence said, pointing. "He's left the door ajar for us. Maybe the buzzer isn't working."

Florence made to push the door open, but my arm rushed out of its own accord, and I caught her by the shoulder. She spun round, surprised. "Oww," she wailed. "What was that for? You almost had my shoulder out its socket."

As if—Florence was such a drama queen.

But I murmured an apology and repeated, "Something's not right. I—I don't think Luca left the door ajar for us."

"Well, why else would it be open?"

"I don't know, but think about it. He's upstairs, two floors away from the street with music playing, and he's happy to leave the side door to his entire shop open? Anyone could walk in and help themselves."

Florence was silent. "People are pretty trusting round here, though. It's not like in London, where I wouldn't dream of leaving the flat door unlocked despite being in a big building with a bolted main entrance. In Broomewode, you'd be more likely to have some sweet tweeting birds steal your knickers off a washing line than experience a break-in."

I shook my head. "I have this bad feeling. I don't know how to explain it."

Florence's brow creased with worry, but despite my warnings, she pulled the door open and called out Luca's name.

No answer.

I shivered again. Now the cold had been replaced by a feverishly hot sensation. I touched my temples and found small beads of sweat there. Oh, this was not good. Not good at all.

Florence disappeared through the doorway. "Come on, Poppy," she called out. "Let's not spook ourselves unnecessarily."

I touched my finger to the cool purple stone around my neck and for the second time that day wished so hard I had Eve's amulet on my wrist. I didn't feel safe without it. I decided the next best thing was to quietly recite the protection spell Eve had given me last week.

Goddesses of the elements four,
Protect us as we go through this door.
Evil keep away, I hereby command.
In safety and comfort, goddesses, hold us safely in your hands.
So I will, so mote it be.

I stepped inside and found myself confronted by a steep spiral staircase that must have once been the servants' stairs when this row of shops belonged to one owner. To my left was a set of double doors that led into the store, to my right a pantry full of stock. The sound of opera was much louder now, and cooking smells wafted down from above. Florence was on the second step of the staircase. She looked at me a little nervously and then called Luca's name once more.

No answer.

We waited another beat.

Nothing.

"Right," I said, trying to draw upon some inner witchy strength. "Let's go up." I pointed to the staircase. "But keep your wits about you. Something doesn't feel right about this."

"Maybe Luca is hurt or sick. We must help him." Florence gave me that nervous look again. So much for her actress confidence.

We climbed the stairs, and I was sure my friend was feeling the same mounting sense of trepidation. Florence was completely silent—such a rare occurrence that it spooked me even further.

As we climbed, the smell of food intensified—rich, earthy basil, roasting garlic. "It's Franco Corelli," Florence whispered, "the opera playing right now, I mean. Luca has very classic taste."

I didn't reply, trying to focus on controlling the electricity coursing through my body. Every nerve was on high alert, and it was taking all my energy not to collapse and tumble down the staircase.

We made it to the top and emerged into a narrow hallway with three doors.

"The music's coming from there," Florence whispered, pointing to the door closest to us. She was right. And according to my nose, that room was also the kitchen.

I knew that if I stood there a second longer I might lose my nerves, so without deliberating, I pushed the door open.

Directly ahead of me was a massive stove with a huge pot on one of the rings, its contents threatening to bubble over.

"Luca?" I called.

Nothing. I went to turn off the gas, and that's when I saw legs and feet jutting out from beneath the kitchen table.

For a moment, the whole world froze. I saw the scene before me like an underexposed photograph, a menacing darkness hovering over the room like a single gray cloud in a bright blue sky. I felt exposed and empty—like my own shadow had suddenly upped and left me.

"No!" I cried, rushing over to the body. "Luca? Can you hear me?" His eyes were closed, and he was still holding a wooden spoon, sauce dripping slowly down.

The only response was the opera singer's melancholy sound

Ma n'atu sole cchiù bello, oi ne',

'o sole mio sta nfronte a te!

I touched my finger to his wrist. It was just as I'd feared.

"No pulse," I said quietly, looking up at Florence.

"You mean, he's...?"

"Dead. Yes."

Her eyes filled with tears. "I don't believe it," she whispered. "He looks like he's only sleeping. Like he could wake up at any moment."

"He must have just passed," I replied. I did a quick sweep of the room to see if his spirit was still here, struggling to make it over to the other side. Nothing. But my eyes were drawn back to the pot that had been bubbling on the stove when we entered the room. I left poor Luca's body and went to investigate.

"Good thinking to turn off the stove."

I shook my head, staring into the pot. I told Florence that the consistency of his pasta sauce would tell us how long Luca had been dead. I motioned for her to join me. "Look," I said. "It's gloopy, which means it's been on the stove too long."

Florence frowned at the mixture, which was an odd brown color, likely from a mixture of chicken stock, wild garlic, and mushroom. Next to the pot was a chopping board loaded with sliced mushrooms as though ready to go into the sauce. Florence looked at me and said, "Those aren't chanterelles."

I squinted at the board. Florence was right. Chanterelles were stocky little things with serrated tops, sort of like cauliflower florets but with an orangey hue. These mushrooms didn't fit the bill at all. "What are they?"

"Oh, Poppy," Florence said, "I'm not positive, but I think they're death caps."

CHAPTER 5

$\mathcal{I}$ stared at the mushrooms on the chopping board. Instead of being part of a healthy, nutritious dinner, the pile of mushrooms looked macabre. Something about their flesh was ghostly. All I saw was a small mountain of misfortune. People died every year from accidentally mistaking poisonous mushrooms for edible ones. It was too terrible.

But Luca was an experienced forager. How could he pick a crop of death caps? Surely being able to identify which mushrooms were poisonous was like rule number one in any budding forager's handbook?

"Do you think he ate some?" Florence asked, her voice rising in pitch.

I nodded. "I imagine they're in the sauce, and tasting it is what killed him."

She made a sound like she was choking. "That could have been us! We were all set to eat this ghastly dish." She pointed at the simmering pot of sauce.

I made to sniff the pot, but Florence pulled me back. "We

don't know what's in there. Surely Luca knew these weren't chanterelles? His whole business is about quality produce. I've never met a man more passionate about mushrooms. He was a connoisseur."

So Florence thought the same way as me. As I looked up from the chopping board to agree with her, I saw that the color from my friend's tanned face had all but disappeared. Her skin was pale and translucent, just a few stubborn freckles peeking through her foundation on either side of her nose.

"I'll call an ambulance and the police, and they'll figure out the cause of Luca's death. It's not up to us. All we'll have to do is give a short, simple statement and then try to put this evening behind us." Even as I was talking, my mind was doing overtime, attempting to figure out how Luca made such a mistake.

But instead of being reassured, Florence looked even more alarmed. She threw up her hands. "The police? Oh no. After last week, I know what that's like. DI Hembly is so thorough. He asks a million questions. Makes you repeat yourself over and over."

"It's his job to get the facts," I said, confused by her sudden attitude. "He has to be thorough."

"Yes, that's very admirable and all, and I'm sure he's a great detective, but the whole ordeal takes forever. I can't lose precious hours to a police investigation. There's too much riding on my performance in the tent tomorrow. I have to be rested and refreshed. I can't be embroiled in a police case. I have to get back to the inn nice and early and get a good night's sleep."

I stared at Florence, my mouth falling open. Was she seriously putting the baking competition above finding out what had happened to her friend? Surely, even Florence could see how self-involved that was.

I raised my eyebrows, as if to say, *You're joking, right?*

But Florence's expression remained deadly serious. "I need to get out of here," she insisted. "Pronto. Please, Poppy, can you do me this one favor? Wait here for the police and then tell them that you were the only one invited to dinner this evening?"

"But we told the others at the pub where we were going. So many people know you're here. It doesn't make sense to lie. Even if I was willing."

"I can say I changed my mind." She looked utterly panicked.

I understood where Florence was coming from—I knew intimately what it was like to want to impress the judges, to be positively burning with that desire. It was all-consuming. No one had more sympathy than me. But there was no way I would lie to the police or compromise an investigation into a death. I told Florence as much, but it was like talking to someone with cotton wool stuffed in their ears—she just wasn't hearing it.

"Why would they ask about me? You won't have to lie. It can't make any difference because you know I didn't kill him. There's simply no point in me getting involved."

Just as I was formulating another argument to explain how crazy her suggestion was, Florence dashed out of the room and raced down the spiral stairs.

Her heels clattered all the way down and then echoed in the cobblestone street.

"You're kidding me," I said to the empty room. I rushed

out onto the landing in time to hear the side door bang close. She was gone.

"That girl is something else," I said into the silence.

I returned to the kitchen and was about to switch off the opera music to call the police when I remembered that touching anything at a potential crime scene was a big no-no. I pulled out my phone and dialed 999.

By now I knew the drill, and when I spoke to the operator, I answered her questions calmly and carefully: The emergency service I needed was the police. The number I was calling from was my own mobile. I waited as she transferred my call to the Force Control Room in Somerset. The new operator asked my location and the nature of the emergency. I was always in awe of how the person at the end of the line never responded with shock or surprise. Their voice was so calm, so steady. I wished I felt more calm and steady right now.

Yes, I was still at the scene, I continued. My emergency was a suspicious death. I gave her my contact details, my address, and place of work. Yes, I could describe what I saw: a dinner abandoned halfway through cooking, a man not long dead prostrate on the floor, wooden spoon in hand. A chopping board of mushrooms that I thought might be poisonous. The operator said that the police were on their way. I needed to stay put to give a statement.

When the call ended, I checked the time. It was eight o'clock, and the sky outside was turning purple like a fresh bruise. I figured it would take a while for the detectives to get to the village and decided a little sleuthing around the building could only help speed up solving the mystery of Luca's death.

I began with the kitchen and went to examine the circular wooden table, which had been all set for dinner. In the center was a vase of peonies, an empty glass water jug, and two silver candelabra sticks with tapered candles, their wicks yet to be lit. Three places had been meticulously set, each with their own woven mat, ceramic pasta bowl, silver knife, fork and spoon, and red wineglass and water tumbler placed to the right. Luca had obviously been used to hosting, and he knew exactly how to lay a welcoming table. Each element had been carefully arranged to anticipate the needs of his guests.

To the right of the table, an antique sideboard stood against the wall. It had a glass cabinet with plates, bowls, and an impressive collection of glasses arranged in rows. On the sideboard sat a bowl filled with bananas, oranges, lemons, and limes. Beside that was an open bottle of red wine. A wineglass about a quarter full sat beside the bottle. I went to inspect the wine more closely. Had Luca been drinking before we arrived and made a big mistake with the mushrooms because he was drunk?

My eyes wandered back up to the glass cabinet. And that's when I noticed that all the wineglasses had been placed drinking side down except for one, which was stem down. It was puzzling. Everything in the kitchen was orderly. Was it a mistake, or did someone drink with him and put the glass back hastily and in the wrong position? I peered into the cabinet, all but pressing my nose against the glass. The lone wineglass had condensation around the rim. It had definitely been recently used and then returned to the cabinet.

Had Luca been enjoying a glass of wine with someone? If so, where were they and why had they put the glass away?

For a moment, I really considered that Luca might have a drinking problem and wanted to conceal that he'd begun the party without us. That would certainly explain why he mistook death caps for chanterelles. But why would he have death caps in the first place? They didn't look a bit like chanterelles. Did they resemble some other mushroom I didn't know about?

Luca presented as jovial and coherent, but I guess you never knew what was really going on under the surface. Florence was on much more friendly terms with the deli owner than I was. It was so frustrating that she'd bolted from the scene. She would have been useful in talking about what she knew of him.

I backed away from the cabinet and decided that I would look for more clues around the apartment. What were the give-aways for someone who drank too much? An excess of mouth-wash? A stash of empty bottles? But before I could get too carried away with my suspicions, a cold sensation spread through my body and all the hairs on the back of my neck stood up until I was chilled to the core. By now, I knew exactly what this was.

I spun round, and sure enough, there was Luca's ghost. He was standing in the doorway, the outline of his body wavy and flickering, a confused expression on his face.

"It's okay," I said softly. "Luca, I'm right here."

"What happened?" he asked, still puzzled. "I feel very funny."

Oh man, Luca had yet to realize what had occurred here tonight. Spirit Luca walked over to where his body lay by the stove. He gasped and clapped a hand to his mouth. "It's me," he murmured. "What am I doing down there?"

"Luca," I said, keeping my voice gentle and reassuring, "your spirit and your body have gone their separate ways. There's nothing to fear. You're safe now."

Luca shook his head, struggling to come to terms with what he was seeing. "But I'm healthy. Fit as a fiddle. My Mediterranean diet saw to that. Olive oil. Lots of fish, red wine, good cheese."

I swallowed. A little drizzle of extra virgin olive oil couldn't have protected him from the scene that went down here tonight. In a quiet voice I said, "I think you were poisoned." I pointed to the chopping board.

Luca looked at me, incredulous—far more shocked than when I'd told him he was a ghost. "Those are not my mushrooms! Those are deadly! What are they doing on my chopping board?"

I told Luca that Florence and I thought he might have picked them accidentally, mistaking the death caps for something else. But he was adamant he'd never make that kind of mistake. "No, this was no accident," he concluded. "If there's one thing I know, it's *fungho.*"

Just as I'd thought. It was kind of handy having a ghost around to actually tell you something about their murder for once.

"Someone was here, weren't they?" I asked him. "Before we arrived?"

But Luca wasn't looking at me; his attention had returned to the sight of his body. He was shaking his head, still mystified. Who could blame him?

I tried again. "Who was here? Who did this to you?"

Finally, Luca tore his gaze away from his body and looked

deeply and soulfully into my eyes. "You must tell Vera I'm sorry."

Vera? Sorry?

And before the final syllable had left his mouth, he pointed ahead, seemingly mesmerized by something invisible to me.

"Luca?" I called out.

His outline began to flicker, and his eyes closed.

"Luca, who is Vera? Why are you sorry?"

His outline flickered with greater vibrancy.

"Stay with me just a second longer—who is Vera?"

But Luca simply smiled softly...and then he faded away.

I let out a long breath. The hairs on my neck, which had prickled and stayed alert from the moment I saw Luca's dead body, now relaxed. My body temperature rose. As much as I was glad not to be burdened with another recent ghost (Gerry was quite enough for me, thank you very much), I lamented not knowing who had visited Luca before he died. Who on earth was Vera? And why did she need an apology?

CHAPTER 6

I exhaled loudly, suddenly exhausted. It wasn't yet
nine, but the roller coaster of the last hour felt like
an entire week had passed since Florence and I had left the
inn. While I'd been searching for clues and trying to get some
answers from Luca's ghost, the sun had set, and I realized that
the only light in the kitchen was the soft orange glow of a
table lamp. I suddenly felt exposed. I was very much alone at
the scene of a heinous crime. *Argh, Pops, why are you always
finding yourself in these precarious situations?* Was I walking
around with a note on my back that read *Looking for Danger?*

And then my mind flashed back to the warning note I'd
received at the inn several weeks ago, when I'd been battling
against my scone demons. Gerry and I had never discovered
who'd authored that cryptic letter, but the words still echoed
in my head, and if I was honest with myself, they spooked
me. The note had urged me to get myself voted off the show,
insisting that Broomewode wasn't safe for me. Before now, I'd
dismissed the note as some jealous nonsense—maybe a
failed baking candidate who never made it through the audi-

tions. But more and more, I wondered if the note had been hinting at the reason I kept coming across murder scenes. As much as the warning had disturbed me, and however hard I'd tried to find who had sent it, I'd also ignored the message completely, trying against all odds to stay in the competition. And now that I'd been voted off the show, I'd continued to ignore the warning and accepted a full-time job that kept me in the village. Had I willingly put myself in the way of grave danger? I wrapped my arms around my middle, willing the police to hurry up and put an end to my vulnerable position.

The ambulance arrived first. I heard the siren and ran downstairs to let the paramedics in, then took them upstairs to Luca. I watched them check him over but already knew he was dead.

Minutes later, I heard a familiar voice calling up the stairs.

"Hello? Anybody in there?"

It was DI Hembly. I answered and was relieved to hear footsteps climb the spiral staircase.

DI Hembly and Sgt. Lane emerged. DI Hembly was dressed smart, as always, in a pristine starched white shirt and navy slacks, his buzz cut precise, his eyes unwavering. Sgt. Lane, younger and more casual, was wearing a similar outfit to his superior, but the look was more hip and more rumpled. They walked into the room and had a quick word with the paramedics, then both came to where I was standing out of the way.

"He's gone," I said quietly.

DI Hembly nodded gravely, and Sgt. Lane shot me a sympathetic look. By now I was used to their different ways of dealing with tragedy. DI Hembly was always formal, from his polished brown brogues to his freshly pressed navy trousers with a careful crease down the middle. DI Hembly was traditional and practical, with a reassuring, no-nonsense approach to solving crime. Never a hair out of place or even a hint of stubble on his chin, DI Hembly could have passed a military inspection.

His partner, Adam Lane, was the yin to his yang. With longish brown hair that curled at the nape of his neck, relaxed white cotton shirts and comfortable-looking slacks, Sgt. Lane was more off-duty chic. Not to mention those adorable dimples.

"My goodness, Poppy," DI Hembly said. "We always seem to be meeting you over dead bodies."

Ouch. "Believe me, I wish we didn't," I said.

Lane was much nicer. "I know this must have been another traumatic evening for you." He paused and waited for a response. Was this their version of good cop/bad cop? What could I say? *Yes, it was crushing, a terrible blow,* but strangely, I was getting used to finding myself in this kind of awful situation. I decided an affirmative noise would suffice.

Sgt. Lane pulled out a notebook. "Would you mind talking us through what happened here this evening?" He led me to a seating area opposite the kitchen and motioned to a chair that would put my back to Luca's body. I appreciated the thoughtfulness, but it wasn't like I was going to forget the sight of the poor man sprawled dead on his kitchen floor.

Before I sat, I glanced back. DI Hembly squatted beside the dining table and looked at the victim and seemed to be studying the area around the corpse. It looked macabre beside the beautifully laid table, where Florence, Luca, and I should have been tucking into a delicious bowl of pasta.

Instead, here I was, being asked to describe the events leading us to the death of the man just meters away. Thank goodness Luca's ghost had made it over to the other side. I couldn't imagine anything more awkward than discussing his death in front of him.

I sat, and Sgt. Lane placed himself in a chair across from me.

"Do you know who that is?"

"Yes." At least we'd started with an easy question. But as I told the sergeant what I knew about Luca, I mulled the problem of Florence. There was no way I could fail to tell the detectives that she was here with me at the scene. There were three places set. Yet doing so would drop her in some seriously hot water. I didn't want to scorch my friend, but I was furious with her, too. She'd put me in such a difficult situation and made herself look positively heartless.

I cleared my throat and began the story leading up to Luca's death and why I was here, at yet another murder scene, starting with the afternoon when Florence and I had bumped into Luca singing opera as he returned from a foraging trip. He'd found a crop of chanterelles he was very excited about cooking and had invited us to dinner.

"Where had he been picking mushrooms?" DI Hembly asked.

I shook my head. Luca had never told us the exact location of his chanterelle patch. I expected he kept very quiet about that secret. "But he did tell us he'd also found wild garlic nearby. That could be a good clue as to where the mushroom patch might be. But to be honest, I'm not sure he picked chanterelles." I gestured at the chopping board, its pile of sliced mushrooms a deathly pyramid. "I'm no expert, but I'm pretty sure those are death caps."

DI Hembly shook his head. "It's amazing how many people we lose to mushroom poisoning every year."

I knew that this wasn't a straightforward case of mushroom poisoning. It was murder. But how could I communicate this to the cops without sounding crazy? It's not like I could tell them Luca had said himself that the mushrooms lying so innocently on the board weren't the ones he'd picked this morning. Could I suggest rooting through his fridge or cupboards to find the real haul of chanterelles? Would that make me sound like I was a marble short of the set? I had a hunch that someone else had been here before me. But all I really had to go on was an upturned glass. When they began investigating, they'd discover he'd been an experienced forager.

I decided to keep my mouth shut and trust the police to do their job. If only I'd been able to ascertain who this Vera person was that Luca wanted to tell he was sorry. Maybe that might have helped me figure out how poisonous mushrooms ended up on his chopping board. Did he think Vera was the one who'd poisoned him? But if that was the case, then why would he want me to tell her he was sorry? Had he wronged Vera and she'd come today to get her vengeance and he'd accepted his fate at her hands? How I would have loved to call him back to get more information, but he was definitely gone. I could feel his spirit had left the building.

"Poppy?" Sgt. Lane looked at me kindly. "You feeling okay?"

Oh dear, I'd been too lost in my thoughts to catch the detective's last question. I gave him a weak smile, wishing I could tell the whole truth. "I'm pretty traumatized. It's been a long day."

Sgt. Lane said he understood. But any kindness there was quickly diminished by DI Hembly's no-nonsense follow-up question. The one I'd been dreading.

"You said you'd been invited to dinner with Florence. But you're here alone," DI Hembly said, stating the obvious.

I swallowed. There's no way I was going to lie for Florence. I thought it was pretty cold that she didn't stay to help solve the mysterious death of a fellow countryman. But I also didn't want to offer up information about my friend. So I told a version of the truth that hopefully made Florence sound a teensy bit sympathetic. "It was very traumatic, discovering his body. Florence, well, she isn't made of stern stuff. She got spooked and ran. I think after her traumatic ordeal last week, she's not fully recovered."

DI Hembly frowned, but Sgt. Lane nodded ever so slightly. "Do you know where she is now?" he asked.

"I think she went back to the inn," I replied. "I'm not really sure. She knows you'll come to speak to her later. I just don't think she could stand staying in the same room as a dead body."

DI Hembly looked at me disapprovingly, as if I could have controlled Florence's behavior. That woman did whatever the heck she wanted.

"I'm sure if you try the inn, she'll be there. She's in room number sixteen," I said, hoping that my help here would bring me back into Hembly's good graces.

But DI Hembly's consternation only seemed to grow deeper. "How is it that you're still here in Broomewode Village, Miss Wilkinson? Weren't you sent home last week?"

So much for keeping the results of the show secret until it was aired. No one was supposed to know who left each week. The detective obviously kept up with local gossip. Nothing was ever really private around here, unless it had to do with my birth parents. And then everyone clammed up!

I swallowed, suddenly feeling like I was on trial. "I was, but Broomewode Inn hired me to make the cakes for afternoon tea and dessert. After what happened to poor Eloise..." I trailed off. What else could I say?

DI Hembly just nodded, but Sgt. Lane congratulated me on my new job. I blushed and thanked him.

People began arriving, officials with a job to do, and the flat quickly became crowded.

"Okay, I think we have enough for now," DI Hembly said. "Sergeant Lane will walk you back to the inn."

"Oh, that's not—" but DI Hembly cut me off in his usual, brusque manner.

"He'll need to talk to Florence."

We left DI Hembly talking to the forensics team. Sgt. Lane would walk me back to the inn and then pay Florence a visit to take her statement. I had no choice, but honestly, it wasn't exactly a hardship to be escorted back to my car, which was in the inn's parking lot, by a handsome detective.

CHAPTER 7

Outside, the evening air was cool, and I shivered in Florence's pink shirt. I suddenly felt silly in her clothes—the blouse wasn't me at all. I would have felt much more comfortable in my plain black T-shirt, flour smudges and all. But I didn't have the brain space to waste on feeling self-conscious. I was happy to be alive, to be safe.

As we walked, the old-fashioned streetlamps cast a soft light, and above, the stars twinkled in the inky sky. Sgt. Lane kept up the interrogation, though he made it seem like we were only chatting. I'd come to know his style, so I wasn't fooled. "You think it's unlikely that your friend Luca would make such a deadly mistake with mushrooms."

"I do. He told us he'd found a patch of chanterelles, but those mushrooms in his kitchen look nothing like chanterelles. I'm not a forager, but even I know that." I wished so hard that I could explain exactly how I knew Luca hadn't picked those mushrooms, but "his spirit told me" didn't exactly have the ring of hard evidence the police were after.

"Did you know him well?"

"No. Not really. I went into his deli with Florence a couple of times for special items, but she knew him better. He often ordered Italian ingredients for her."

"And yet he invited you to his home for dinner?"

I didn't want to throw Florence under the bus, but I wasn't going to lie to the police, either. "He invited Florence and, since I was standing beside her at the time, he included me in the invitation."

"And he and Florence. Were they close?"

It took me a second to get what he meant. "Romantically, you mean? No. Nothing like that. She liked him for his produce."

"So you didn't know him at all?"

"I know he loved to sing and had an amazing voice." I knew he wanted to tell Vera he was sorry. "He and Florence chatted in Italian, but I'm not sure when he came to this country."

"Any idea why he settled in Broomewode?"

Until Sgt. Lane asked, I'd never thought that it was an odd location for Luca to choose to live in. Broomewode wasn't very international, apart from the baking contestants, or a hub of foodies. I shook my head.

"I'm sure I don't need to tell you to be careful. If you're right and he didn't make a mistake with those mushrooms, then there could be a killer on the loose."

It was nice that Adam Lane was worried about my safety, but I had Team Poppy looking out for me. At last count I had Gateau, Sly, a mysterious hawk, and an entire coven of witches on my side. Not too shabby for a young witch.

When we reached the inn, Adam extended his hand to shake mine as we parted ways in the hall. I felt like I was part of the police crew, and perhaps I had a friend in Adam, too. A quick check of the dining room showed all the baking contestants, including Florence, had left. No doubt they were all getting an early night. I watched as he climbed the stairs, and I hoped Florence would forgive me for telling the police she'd been with me when we discovered Luca's body. As cold as she'd been, and as disappointed as I was in her behavior, I didn't want to mess up her chances this weekend.

As soon as he was out of sight, I went straight to Eve, grateful to see her kind, smiling face serving behind the bar. She was standing next to the new girl, instructing her how to pour the perfect pint. The young woman frowned in concentration, her long red hair pulled back in a braid similar to Eve's gray one. She was wearing a white shirt with a Victorian-style brocade collar—charming but very impractical for a shift behind a busy bar. She was probably younger than I was and visibly nervous. I could see her hands shaking, and she wore several gold bands on her fingers. But if anyone could put the new hire at ease, it was Eve—she knew how to make anyone feel at home, witch or not. Though probably best if she not share too much about Darius, the man this young woman was replacing.

The moment she saw me, Eve's soft expression changed. She gestured for me to come forward and take a seat at one of the empty stools at the corner of the bar.

"Now that's it, Philly. Make sure the ale has a slightly frothy head. Gentle does it, gently now. Don't spook the pint."

I had to stifle a small giggle. Eve sounded like she was helping her new protégé herd a flock of sheep. I watched as Philly finished the pint and put it carefully down in front of a customer at the other end of the bar.

Eve turned her attention to me and asked what had happened. Why was I back here so early, and why did my face have that ominous expression on it?

I settled on the stool, and in hushed tones I explained the tragedy that had befallen Luca, the whole mushroom mix-up, Florence fleeing, my statement to the police. I wanted to share Luca's cryptic parting message before he crossed to the other side, but that would have to wait. I couldn't take any chances with eavesdroppers. The inn was too crowded.

"Oh, Poppy. Not again."

I nodded.

Eve, usually so calm, looked sickened. "I should have known," she said in despair.

"What could you have known?"

"The energy levels in the village are all off. Something bad is brewing in Broomewode. And with all the warnings you've had to stay away... What if you'd disturbed the murderer at the scene? You could have been in awful danger, Poppy."

I told Eve it wasn't her fault. There was no way she could have prevented the wicked forces at work. Who was to know that a simple dinner invitation would end in murder?

But Eve didn't look reassured. "You must sleep at the inn tonight, love. There's no way I'll let you drive back to the cottage on your own in the dark."

I wanted to protest. My own bed seemed like bliss to me right now, and I missed Gateau. But Eve sounded just like Sgt. Lane, except that she knew I had witch powers and still she didn't want me to drive home alone. Maybe that meant I shouldn't take my chances. I trusted Eve's instincts, and I was pretty rattled. Maybe driving wasn't the best idea. Gateau had one of those endless food contraptions, plenty of water, and a cat door. We'd miss each other, but she'd be fine.

"But staff aren't meant to sleep in the rooms," I said. "Will it be okay?"

She nodded. "After what you've been through? Of course. No one would want to take risks with your safety. How would we forgive ourselves if something ever happened to you, dear Poppy?" She took a room key from its little hook and pressed it into my hand. "Your old room hasn't been booked this weekend. It's like it was meant to be. Now you could do with a drink, I'm sure."

"I'll get that," a man's voice said.

I turned round and was surprised to see Benedict. He was dressed more casually than usual in a white linen shirt and dark jeans, his hair a little messy. He looked tired.

"I heard what happened to Luca," he said, taking the stool next to me.

Did nothing stay quiet around here?

"It was terrible," I said.

"Awful business. I thought you might be here, so I came to see if you're okay."

Benedict was a constant puzzle. When I'd first arrived, he'd been cold, rude, and seemed bent on getting rid of me, but lately he seemed to seek out my company. Or was I imagining things? I'd definitely seen a nicer side to him over the past few weeks.

I thanked him, then retold the details I'd just passed on to Eve—but not before asking for a red wine. I watched with a little glee as Eve reached for the most expensive bottle and poured me a hefty measure. "I'll put that on your tab," she said to Benedict. "And your usual ale?"

He nodded, and Eve pulled him a pint, placing it on a beer mat next to my wine. "You'll be needing some substance, too, Poppy. You've not had any dinner, either. What about some soup?"

"I couldn't eat."

She excused herself, as there was a yelp of distress from Philly at the other end of the bar.

"I haven't eaten either," Benedict said. "Why don't we order a few things and see if we can get some food down?"

I turned to Benedict, who was taking a long pull of his ale. "That's a great idea." I shuddered. "Anything but pasta. Or mushrooms." I suspected it would be a while before I ate a mushroom.

We both scanned the board, and when Eve returned, we asked for a salad, a cheese plate, and a plate of chips, aka french fries. I knew I should eat, and hopefully with Eve and Benedict to chat to, I could keep my mind off death long enough to get some food down.

She nodded, approving, and put the order in.

"You know, I saw Luca earlier today," Benedict said. "I was out on estate business, and he was foraging."

I told him that I'd seen him, too, and that he'd invited Florence and me over to sample his chanterelle and wild garlic pasta. That was how I'd found him dead.

Benedict shook his head sadly. "That man had an amazing knack for sniffing out chanterelles. It was like he had a second nose for it."

My eyes widened. "Was that something people knew about Luca? That he had a particular talent for finding mushrooms?"

"Oh yes. He always swore he'd never share his secret patch."

Eve returned with our food. I nibbled a piece of cheese, and Benedict dunked a fry into the pot of homemade mayo that I'd watched Pavel make earlier.

"There's no way that Luca would have mistaken death caps for chanterelles, is there?" I asked.

"Not a chance,'" Benedict said decisively, taking another long drink of his ale. "Luca was the one who showed *other* people which mushrooms were poisonous. He was incredibly knowledgeable and dedicated to learning about the land. And he especially knew about chanterelles. They were his favorite."

"But they were in a secret place?"

Benedict laughed. "I mean, he said they were secret, but he had a habit of singing when he was foraging, so his findings were never as secret as he thought. All a person would have to do is follow the sound of his latest aria." He paused, clearly saddened. "Luca was a talented man."

I agreed, but my mind was working at a mile a minute. If it wasn't a one-off today that Luca was walking through the Broomewode estate singing, then this would make it easy for a killer to stalk him and find where all the different mushroom breeds grew in the grounds. Luca could have sung for his poisoned supper. I stared into my glass of wine as if I could find the answers there.

"You look very worried, Poppy," Benedict said softly and touched my arm.

That was weird. I felt a buzz of electricity. I glanced up, and he took his hand back. I asked aloud the questions I'd been worrying about. "Who would want Luca dead? And did the killer know Florence and I were coming for dinner?" No doubt I was being paranoid, but what if Luca hadn't sampled his sauce as he was cooking? What if he'd served dinner tonight as promised? There could have been three bodies on Luca's kitchen floor. One of them mine.

"The police will find out whether this was more than an unlucky accident, Poppy. I don't want you to put yourself in harm's way," he continued. "I hope it won't put you off Broomewode. We've become used to having you here, like you belong."

I looked at Benedict, amazed. No one had ever said they thought I belonged here. In fact, I'd been getting the opposite messages—leave, get away, get out, you're in danger. I was suffused with a warm feeling of affection for Benedict. He made me feel accepted. I thanked him for his words.

"You've no idea what that means to me," I said quietly. "From the first time I stepped foot in Broomewode, it's felt like home to me."

"And me," Benedict said, smiling. He held my gaze. It was one of those moments, like time might slow down and he'd ease forward until our lips met. Then he suddenly dropped his gaze, finishing his pint in one fell swoop. "Must be getting off," he said. "Early morning tomorrow. Good to see you safe, Poppy."

And just like that, he left.

I finished up my wine, waved to Eve, who was busy with Philly, and went to my locker to fetch the toiletry bag I kept there along with the last clean T-shirt. Then I headed to my old bedroom. Despite my earlier hesitancy, I was happy to trundle upstairs and not have to drive home after such a long day. I was looking forward to running a hot, deep bath, throwing in some scented bubbles and then falling into a well-deserved sleep before my painfully early shift tomorrow.

But of course, nothing could be easy, could it?

As I turned the key in the lock, there was my faithful companion. Not Gateau, but Gerry, who clearly had other plans for me that did not involve peace and quiet.

Gerry had formed himself into a perfect circle and rested against my door like a ghoulish Christmas wreath. I jumped at the unexpected sight but luckily didn't cry out.

"Gotcha!" he cried, pleased with himself. Then he melted into the room, and I unlocked the door and went through.

"How did you know I was going to be here?" I asked, locking the door behind me.

Gerry turned and grinned that broad, toothy smile of his. "I was floating about in the bar, just minding my own business like, and I overheard you and Broomewode's most eligible bachelor talking."

I couldn't believe I'd not spotted Gerry downstairs. Were my senses failing me? "Gerry. Do you know the meaning of privacy?"

"Yes, I do, but remember I'm your guardian ghost, Pops. It's like literally my duty to snoop on you."

"Too bad you couldn't follow me to Broomewode Village tonight and protect me."

I ran through the events of the evening. Gerry was agog, following the twists and turns, but his expression fell as I described Luca's final cryptic message before he passed over.

He sighed. "I don't get it, Pops. Everyone else seems to manage it. Why can't I move on?"

"I don't know." I truly wished I had the answers for Gerry.

"When Luca finished giving me his message, it looked as if his eyes were trained on something in front of him."

"That light you were talking about last week at the witches' circle?"

"Exactly. It was like there was a light there, something leading him. Surely there must be a light for you somewhere. What about in the tent? Can you not go towards the light?"

"I don't see any light," he wailed. "Believe me, I'd be running towards it with arms wide open if I did."

"We'll try again," I promised. I wanted peace for Gerry as much as he did. Not to mention a little peace for myself.

I shooed Gerry out and ran myself a bath, rinsing out my underwear for the morning while I waited for the bath to fill.

CHAPTER 8

*I*n spite or maybe because of the dramatic events, I slept like a newborn, lost in a world of strange dreams, none of which I could make sense of as my alarm shook me awake from that other world. At least spending the night at the inn meant that I got a bit longer in bed. However, at five a.m., my alarm squealed, and I reached out for Gateau, only to remember she was tucked up at my cottage. How I missed my sweet familiar. I hoped she and Mildred weren't getting up to any mischief while I was gone.

I put myself under the hot shower, moisturized, and dressed in yesterday's clothes, apart from my last clean T-shirt. I set aside Florence's shirt to give back to her later. A quick lick of mascara and lip balm, and then I pulled up my hair into a practical bun, ready for the morning rush getting the breakfast pastries ready. Somehow I was going to have to turn my mind away from Luca and back towards cake.

I walked downstairs sleepily and entered the inn's kitchen, desperate for some coffee. Sol was already there and offered his usual grunt of a hello. He wasn't much of a morning person either, but he made excellent coffee. The sharp, sweet scent permeated the kitchen. I helped myself, still half stuck in slumber.

I turned on my proofing oven and the baking ovens and then went to the fridge to pull out the dough I'd prepared yesterday. The overhead lights bounced off of the immaculate stainless-steel worktops, gas ranges, and fridges, making the space appear even bigger than it was in reality, playing tricks with the space.

"Thought I'd make rhubarb Danish with the fresh rhubarb Susan Bentley gave me yesterday," I said, fetching the rhubarb from the fridge.

"Suit yourself." He said that, but he kept a close eye on what I was doing. "You'd better make an extra chocolate and hazelnut torte. It was so popular, they ran out yesterday." It didn't sound like a compliment, but coming from Sol, him letting me know my torte had been popular was a pat on the back.

As usual, everything was gleaming. Sol was a stickler for cleanliness, so anytime the kitchen didn't smell of delicious cooking, the scent of lemon surface spray tickled my nose. I couldn't believe that it was only last week that I'd felt a tinge of jealousy that Eloise baked in such a well-equipped and spacious kitchen. Now I'd taken her place. I was finding it difficult not to compare myself to the unfortunate girl or to feel her spirit watching over me. But at least I knew she had passed over to the other side peacefully. I just hoped I could honor her legacy of delicious bakes. I felt duty-bound to make sure I was up to scratch.

And now it was my job—my job!—to bake the morning muffins for breakfast service. The plan was to make a mix of lemon and poppy seed, and blueberry. I also had croissants to bake fresh, and we always added something special so returning guests had something different to try. Rhubarb Danish, this morning.

I topped up my coffee and got to work.

Pavel arrived and joined Sol in the prep for cooked breakfast. The two of them worked in comfortable silence, the sound of the local radio station providing soft background noise. News of Luca's death was the top story, but the details released to the media were scant and soon gave way to the trouble caused by an escaped flock of sheep from a farm six miles away. Sol and Pavel expressed their shock about Luca. I thought about sharing what I knew about what had happened last night, but I decided against it. The police would share the details in their own time.

I went into autopilot, and before long, the Danish were cooked and emitting the most wonderful fragrance of pastry and rhubarb. I sprinkled a little pearl sugar around the edges of the Danish as they were cooling. Both muffin batters were mixed and ready to go into the ovens. I put the muffins in the oven and wished them well.

While they bubbled away, rising slowly but surely, I helped the men with the arrangement of the breakfast buffet. We served cereals and granola, individual fruit yogurt pots supplied by the local dairy, sliced cheeses and cold cuts, jams and preserves for toast, and great heated trays of crispy streaky bacon and scrambled eggs. It was a lot to carry, even with three people. The pub was already filling up with early risers (who were these people, and why did they get up so early!), and I felt a glow of pride that I was part of it. I arranged the muffins, croissants, and rhubarb Danish on a big ceramic platter and took them out.

Once the big items were out, I arranged the fruit bowl and returned to the kitchen to devour one of Sol's famous bacon sandwiches.

I bit into the sandwich with glee—a salty, carby treat was just what I needed to face the rest of the day. I was on a split shift, which meant I'd be on a break for a few hours before coming back to prepare cakes for afternoon tea. The lunchtime desserts were already prepped, thank goodness. The life of a professional pastry chef was certainly full-on. It was almost as exhausting as preparing for a weekend of filming for *The Great British Baking Contest*.

Having obliterated my sandwich, I went to check the buffet table, taking some of the still-warm muffins in a basket to replenish the plate.

It was going to take a while to get into the rhythm of this job, but the satisfaction factor was high. I had gone from being an amateur baker to a professional and was quite proud of myself.

As I turned to survey the early breakfasters, to my surprise, I saw Florence. I couldn't believe she was up and dressed at this early hour, packing herself a take-away breakfast. She looked as gorgeous as ever in a rust-colored shirt and wide-legged black trousers, her hair pulled away from her face in a swinging ponytail. She stifled a yawn, clearly tired, although her makeup was pristine, tiny black flicks at the corners of her eyes lending her a feline look.

I walked to her table, wondering how she was going to greet me after I went against her wishes and told the police she'd fled the scene of a murder.

Florence saw me and waved. Was she angry? It was hard to tell. Florence was so friendly and warm, but after last night, I knew that she had it in her to be brutally cold. I joined her at the corner table, ready to receive some kind of ticking off, but Florence apologized before I even opened my mouth.

"I know you must think I'm a terrible person," she said, arranging her features into the most contrite expression. "But I think I just spooked. After everything with Darius last week, well, I just couldn't stomach any more drama. And before you say anything, yes, I know I normally live for drama, but this was more than even I could take."

"I understand," I said truthfully. "But you did put me in an awkward position. I had to tell the truth."

Florence nodded. "Sergeant Dreamy Dimples knocked on my door not long after I got back. I'll admit my first thought was that all my wildest dreams had come true, but I soon realized he was there strictly on business. More's the pity."

Trust Florence to use a police investigation as an opportunity to flirt wildly with a detective.

"Anyway, I told him that I was with you but the whole thing had just been too much after last week and I thought you'd be able to handle the report without me. He was pretty understanding but asked me a hundred questions anyway. It went on for ages—which explains these bags." She pointed to her eyes. They looked perfect to me.

"He had to do his job," I said, shrugging.

"Luckily, I was still able to catch some much-needed beauty sleep. Today's a big day, as you well know. Speaking of which"—Florence began walking to the door—"I need to get going. It took a herculean effort to get up this early. I want to settle into the tent, arrange my ingredients, practice my lines." But as she turned towards the door, I noticed a brown package tucked underneath her arm.

She saw my eyes drawn to the package and shuffled to hide it from view.

Oh, not so fast. "What is that?" I asked.

She paused, clearly making up her mind if she wanted to act her way through this or actually tell the truth. But I already knew what I was looking at, and it horrified me.

"Florence?" I said, lending my voice a disapproving edge. "Is that bag from Luca's deli? Surely you didn't manage to pick up the ingredients last night after we found his dead body!"

"Really, Poppy, I have to get going—" she started, but I cut her off.

"Did you rummage through the store before you left last night? Before his body was even cold?"

Florence looked at me aghast. "Of course not. How could you even think such a thing?"

She looked down at her watch pointedly.

"I'll walk with you," I said firmly, "and you can talk freely without worrying about the time."

Florence frowned, but there was nothing she could say to deter me, and she knew it. We left the inn and emerged into the early morning sunshine. Birds were singing. The sun was glinting off the white roof of the baking tents. It was going to be hot in there today. I was a little sad not to be part of the craziness but also somewhat relieved. And today I had more on my mind than baking.

"The package?" I asked.

"All right. I popped down to Luca's deli before we went to

dinner."

"You did? Why didn't you say so?"

Florence shrugged. "I didn't think it was important. I was kind of antsy to get my hands on the ingredients, you know. I figured that I'd end up drinking too much red wine at dinner and forget to pick up the vanilla beans and almond paste and then my recipe would be ruined. This is really important to me, Poppy."

I understood her wanting to do well today, but it seemed a little strange she'd left out that detail last night. Florence insisted she'd forgotten and asked me to drop the subject—she'd had enough questioning from Sgt. Lane last night. But there was no way I was going to let this go.

"What time were you at the deli?" I asked.

She let out an irritated sigh. "About four p.m., I think. It was still really warm. I was sweating a bit and was worried about getting pit stains on my shirt."

Trust Florence to remember the details about her appearance. I tried to disguise my annoyance. Did she really not realize that anything she did or saw yesterday could be helpful in a murder investigation? I swallowed and took a breath. "Did you see anything unusual when you were there? Anyone loitering around the store or behaving suspiciously?"

Florence shook her head. "No, there was only one other customer there, a woman. She was a bit of a pain, to be honest, umming and ahhing over some serrano ham. I mean, it's just ham. Buy the most expensive one and get out of there."

A woman? Could that have been the mysterious Vera that Luca wanted to say sorry to? Was Vera the last person to see Luca alive?

"Did you catch her name?" I asked. "Could you describe her?"

"Not a name, no, although Luca appeared to be as frustrated with her as I was. She was quite old, gray-haired. I'd never seen her before. She had this high, squeaky voice that went right through me."

Was that someone Luca might want to apologize to? Someone he'd known in the past? I asked if the woman had an Italian accent, but Florence just looked at me like I'd shot a baby duckling.

"Of course not," she practically spat. "Any Italian worth their Guccis would know exactly what kind of ham they wanted from the deli."

Oof, forgive me for asking!

"Was anyone else around?"

Florence shook her head and picked up her pace. She was obviously becoming irritated with me, but if she'd told me all this yesterday, then she could have avoided this interrogation pre-competition.

"No," she said. "But I did see a woman on my way back to the inn who might have been heading to the deli. I only noticed her because she was carrying a Dionigi."

"A Dionigi?" I had no idea what that might be. An animal of some sort? A plant?

"Really, Poppy. It's a handbag. They're ever so famous and exclusive. Made in Milano, though of course hers would have been a knockoff fake."

Of course, Florence had noticed the woman's purse. "Anything else?"

She flapped her hand. "Some papers close to her chest, like she was protecting them from something."

"Papers? Like newspaper?"

"No. White pages with musical notes."

"Sheet music?" That would make sense with Luca's singing background. Maybe he was taking singing lessons? Or giving them?

Again, Florence shrugged. "Probably. I didn't really pay attention."

Hmm, she didn't seem too interested in getting to the bottom of Luca's murder. Even so, I persisted. "Could you describe her? Anything at all distinguishing about her appearance."

"She had lovely blond hair, as a matter of fact. A very well-cut lob."

"Lob?"

"You know, a long bob, swingy, almost to the shoulders, that kind of thing. But she ruined the elegant effect with a pair of pants which ended at her calves, which I also happened to notice, with no disrespect intended, were the shape of cantaloupes."

I wondered what she said about me behind my back and was fairly happy not to know.

We were nearing the competition tent, and I stopped in my tracks. I so did not want to turn up there so soon after getting booted out. That would *not* be a cool look. I thanked Florence for the (somewhat belated) information and wished her luck for the day.

She waved goodbye merrily, looking pretty carefree for someone who'd found a dead body the previous night. My gut was churning and my emotions running riot. I'd been understanding when Florence bolted from the murder scene last night, but discovering she'd been at the scene of the crime only a couple of hours before and neglected to tell me...well, it didn't sit right.

It occurred to me that Luca and Florence were the only two Italians in Broomewode as far as I knew. And she'd been one of the last people to see Luca alive.

Coincidence?

Or not?

CHAPTER 9

I headed back to the inn, wishing I'd been able to get something more concrete from Florence. Was she hiding something from me? Why? Had there been something going on between her and Luca? Just the thought made me grimace. Surely, he was too old for her. Although with Florence, you never knew. She'd sworn off men only yesterday but seemed pretty at ease flirting with Adam Lane, the detective, last night. I thought again about how eager Florence had been to accept Luca's dinner invitation. She'd dismissed her enthusiasm as that of a pasta lover, but could there be other types of love at play here beyond a bowl of carbs?

I thought about all I knew about Luca. It wasn't much. He ran a deli specializing in Italian delicacies; he had a beautiful singing voice; he loved to forage; he'd discovered a secret patch of chanterelles that he was very proud of; he was welcoming and generous with food, and a woman with blond hair who *might* have something to do with his musical life *might* have visited yesterday. Or the woman was just a coincidence. Hmm, it wasn't really much to go on.

I picked up my pace. Eve would have arrived for work by now. I wanted to ask if she knew anything about Luca's singing. Did he give lessons on the side? Or belong to a group, perhaps? Any small detail could be the key to solving this mystery, and I felt I owed it to Luca's spirit to come good on his last wish.

The sun shone down as I raced back along the now familiar path to the inn. Blotches of light burst through the bushy leaves of whitebeam trees and cast dappled patterns on the ground. If only everything in Broomewode was this beautiful. I sighed, trying to shake the feeling that maybe I didn't know my friend as well as I thought. I felt more grateful than ever for the Broomewode coven that I'd discovered since I first arrived for filming. I needed my sisters' expertise and support during this tumultuous week, what with my new job and another murder. I needed to be able to put my trust in the people around me.

Inside the inn, I breathed a sigh of relief to catch a flash of Eve's silver braid as she bent to unload the glasswasher. The early-bird breakfast crowd had all but disappeared, and there were a few tables (mostly of sleepy-looking couples) left, sipping tea and reading the papers. I beamed with pride as I watched one of the guests bite into her lemon and poppy-seed muffin. By her expression, it was delicious. At least there was one thing I could get right.

I rushed over to Eve and greeted her with a great big bear hug, the usual jolt of electricity coursing through my body as I squeezed her tight. Eve laughed and asked what all the fuss was about.

"I'm so pleased to see you," I said. "You were a lifesaver last night, calming me down, feeding me."

Eve smiled and said that's what sisters do for each other. "Mind you, I think most of your comfort last night came from another, more male source." She grinned wickedly.

I gasped. "Eve! What are you insinuating?"

"Nothing. I'm only saying, little sister, that the two of you are a good influence on each other. You bring Benedict back down to earth where he belongs, and believe it or not, he does the exact same for you."

I felt my mouth drop open. "You think my head is in the clouds?"

Eve flipped her braid over her shoulder and looked me right in the eye. "Come on, Poppy, you're always getting caught in dark dramas, rushing off and putting yourself in danger. Having Benedict around the last couple of weeks has been to your benefit, has it not? He's sensible and grounded. Something I believe you stand in need of."

I was shocked. I mean, I knew that Benedict had been kind lately, not haughty or judgmental like he'd been when we first met. But a good influence? Him? On me? As if.

Eve laughed again. "Close your jaw, dear. You'll catch flies that way."

I snapped my jaw shut, too stunned to protest further. I was just going to have to gracefully ignore Eve's teasing.

"And I've seen the way that detective looks at you," Eve said.

"Adam?" I asked, incredulous.

She nodded, a wicked grin on her face. "First-name basis, are we?"

I went crimson. Why was my love life (or lack of it)

suddenly so interesting? "We just know each other from investigations. Nothing more to it than that."

"Is that why he escorted you back here last night? I saw the two of you while I was taking out the trash. But, if my two cents is worth anything, then why land a sprat when you could reel in a mackerel. Know what I mean?"

I definitely didn't. I had no interest in fishing for men. A change of subject was in order.

I cleared my throat. "Anyway, I wanted to ask—Luca had a beautiful singing voice. I was wondering, where would someone who loved to sing go in Broomewode? Was he part of a group? Or involved in amateur dramatics, maybe? A musical?"

"Yes, he was in the church choir," Eve said. "You should ask Susan about it. She and Reginald are also in the choir. She's at the market this morning, but I'm sure she'll be back later."

The church choir. That probably involved sheet music.

Maybe the woman Florence saw with sheet music was the choirmaster? I'd have to visit the church before the next half of my shift started. I only hoped there'd be someone there I could talk to. Work was a blessing, but it did get in the way of making progress on a murder investigation.

But before I could ask Eve any more questions, Jonathon Pine and Elspeth Peach swept into the room. Everyone's heads turned to look at the famous duo. Did they ever get used to that level of attention? It would drive me mad, being recognized everywhere I went. Not that I had to worry—my job was the very definition of behind the scenes. However, this season of *The Great British Baking Contest* hadn't aired yet. But when it did, millions of viewers would be tuned in, following my every baking move. I'd already been warned that I'd be recognized by complete strangers on the street. When I'd applied for the show, I really hadn't given that aspect of the competition much thought. I'd been focused on getting through the tough auditions so that I had an excuse to snoop around the village where I might have been born and try to get close to the staff at Broomewode Hall.

Only now was I considering having to face the actual consequences of being on TV. Every silly thing I said or did would have been captured on camera. And who knew how I was going to be edited? What if the editing team took a disliking to me? Decided that I was going to be the arrogant one, or clumsy one, or the one who thought she was better than she actually was. I had no control over what scenes would be shown or which would be cut. How would I come across to the general public? Would they love me or loathe me? ARGH. It was too troubling to think about. I needed to stop this train of thought pronto.

Luckily, Elspeth spotted me at the bar and waved, breaking my horrible reverie. She looked lovely as always, entirely camera-ready in an elegant cream twin set and her hair styled in a chignon. Jonathon had donned a blue shirt that complemented his piercing blue eyes.

"So glad we caught you, Poppy," Elspeth said warmly as she glided towards me. "We're heading to the tent, but we heard about last night. Honestly, it sends ice into my heart knowing that you were in danger...again."

"We're very worried," Jonathon said grimly. His eyes took on an intensity I'd never seen before. "We have a duty to protect you, Poppy."

I was touched. And maybe even a little spooked. Was I

really in all that much danger? After all, I'd discovered Luca's body—that wasn't exactly being embroiled in a murder. I said as much to them both, but they shot me down, simultaneously dismissing my point.

"You were the first to arrive at the scene of the crime," Elspeth said softly. "What if you'd disturbed the killer in the act? I couldn't bear it if something happened to you. Didn't you sense danger?"

I had, and my fingers automatically reached up to rest on the amethyst necklace Elspeth had given me. I knew she'd imbued it with protective powers.

Her eyes followed the movement of my hand. "I'm glad to see you're wearing the stone," Elspeth said. "It will do you much good, but it can't protect you from all the evil forces which work in the world."

I nodded solemnly. Jonathon and Elspeth hadn't been so outwardly friendly or, indeed, caring while I was in the competition, but I guessed now our connection was the coven, not cakes, and they were able to be a little freer with their affection.

"In fact," Elspeth continued, her buttery voice softening even further, "as happy as we are about your job here, Poppy, and however nice it is for us to have you around, which it is —" She stopped and glanced at Jonathon, who nodded obediently. "We thought perhaps it might be a good idea for you to stay away from Broomewode Village for the time being. There have been too many near-misses with you."

My heart dropped into my sneakers. Elspeth wanted me to leave? After everything I'd told her about the search for my birth parents? She'd been the first person I'd confided in about my ability to see ghosts and about why I was really here. I trusted Elspeth implicitly, with my life even, and now she was telling me to go? To give up? How could she even suggest this when she knew how much staying meant to me? I hung my head, disappointed and despondent.

"Don't take this the wrong way," Jonathon insisted, as if there was any other way for me to take it. "We'd love to see more of you. But even with amethysts, amulets, and protection spells, all the signs are pointing to danger." He hesitated. "I had a vision that disturbed me. You were in danger, and we couldn't reach you."

"Yes," Elspeth said kindly but firmly. "My senses are quivering, too. There's danger in the air." She patted my shoulder. "Please be careful and do try to stay out of trouble. You really should think about leaving." And then she glanced at the big clock on the wall. "And now we must be off to judge desserts."

CHAPTER 10

J stared after the two contest judges—and witches. Elspeth's and Jonathon's witchy senses were quivering, and everything was pointing towards danger. Danger for me! It was *so* not what this witch wanted to hear. Was I in real danger? Maybe I'd been naïve to think that Team Poppy could deal with the heavy lifting round here. Plus, there was whoever had sent me the warning note, telling me to leave.

And yet, the more people told me to leave, the more stubbornly I felt I needed to stay put. Danger wouldn't go away because I did. It would go away when it was defeated.

"Don't listen to them, Pops," Gerry said, floating down from where he'd been hovering above our heads. "They don't know you've got a guardian ghost on duty."

"Thanks, Gerry," I said, glad to have someone who wanted me to stay, even if I suspected his reasons were selfish. He was lonely without me to play to. "But you can't go farther than the competition tent."

He did a double flip and landed gracefully in front of me.

"Then stay here and you'll be fine. Also, didn't the boy detective hand you his card last night?"

I gaped at Gerry. "You saw that?"

"I keep my eyes open."

It was true. Adam Lane had given me a business card with his personal mobile number on it last night before we parted ways. He'd pressed it into my palm, saying it was in case of an emergency. "You might need someone to come quickly," he'd said, "someone with training who can act fast." I'd thanked him, surprised as anything but also extremely thankful. It warmed my heart to know that Adam had my back. He was a good man, and the more time I spent in Broomewode, the more I realized that was a seriously rare commodity.

I was about to seek some comfort from Eve when Susan walked in, all the bright, boisterous spark drained from her face. She was wearing green overalls, and her hair looked as if it hadn't yet been brushed. Eve immediately left the bar and went to embrace her friend.

"Everything okay?" I asked tentatively.

"I need to be near my sisters after hearing what happened to Luca. I was dropping honey at the farmer's market and decided to come straight here rather than going home alone. What an awful, awful business."

Eve said she'd make us all a cappuccino, and I patted the seat next to me, putting an arm around my friend's shoulders. As much as I wanted to get to the church and try to speak with the choirmaster, I knew that sisters had to come first. Besides, if Susan was upset about Luca, maybe she'd share what she knew about him so we could make progress on solving his murder. Not that I was going to lead with that question. Susan had experienced enough suffering in the short time I'd known her. She leaned against me, and she smelled like honey, such a sweet smell in the middle of this dark news.

I pulled away from Susan, and she took out an embroidered handkerchief to dab at her face. She smiled at me sadly and apologized for letting her emotions get the better of her.

"Don't be silly," Eve said, pausing from her barista duties. "It's good to let your emotions run free. Never does a person good to hide what they're feeling."

I lowered my voice even though there was hardly anyone in the dining room, apart from Gerry, who was doing a handstand atop the barista machine, but he already knew. I admitted that I had been the one who found Luca.

Susan's expression suddenly turned from sadness to alarm. "You did?"

I nodded grimly.

"Poppy!" she exclaimed. "There's so little official news, but the rumor is he was poisoned."

Interesting. "What have you heard?"

Susan shook her head. "Luca and I are part of the Broomewode Foraging Group. Someone posted on our online message board this morning that he died. I couldn't believe it. Normally I go on there to check for tips about finding plants that won't grow on my land. But this morning I got such terrible news. Then, at the farmer's market, a woman selling home-grown flowers said she'd heard he died of poisoning. That's all I know. And you know what village gossip is like. He could have died of hundreds of other causes."

Eve set a black Americano in front of me and a cappuccino for Susan. I loved how she knew our tastes without even asking. She made herself an espresso and joined us. I took a sip of the perfectly brewed coffee before recounting the events of last night, telling Susan that Luca had invited Florence and I over for dinner after we bumped into him and his freshly picked chanterelles.

Susan smiled sadly. "We had many a chat about cooking with foraged food. He often came and picked herbs from my garden. He famously had a secret spot for chanterelles he'd never share, but anyone who cared to follow his loud singing could find it easily enough."

"That's exactly how we bumped into him!" I said, not surprised to hear again that Luca's secret spot was not so secret after all. "Florence and I were walking back from your place yesterday with the eggs when we heard this amazing singing, and then he burst out of the woods and appeared in front of us."

She nodded. "That sounds like Luca." She sipped her own coffee. "And very like him to have then invited you to share his feast."

My mind began to work overtime. If Susan's foraging group knew that Luca had a secret spot for chanterelles, surely that would help the police understand there was no way he'd mistake death caps for his favorite type of mushroom?

I quickly filled Susan in on the rest of last night. How Florence bolted, the wineglass put back the wrong way, the chopping board with sliced mushrooms that looked like death caps and then finally how Luca's ghost had hung around just long enough to pass on his cryptic final words.

Susan exhaled loudly. "Oh my."

"I know, right? It doesn't add up."

"Certainly not. There's simply no way he'd make that kind of mistake with mushrooms," Susan exclaimed. "A death cap might be confused with a European white egg mushroom, but not with a chanterelle. And not by Luca."

This was exactly the kind of reaction I'd hoped Susan would have. If she could provide a statement to the police that recounted Luca's deep knowledge of the land and its produce, then that could help convince them to investigate his death as a murder.

"His last words were to tell Vera he was sorry. Do either of you know who Vera is?"

Eve shook her head. "Don't know of any Vera living locally."

Susan didn't either.

"Did Luca have a girlfriend? An estranged family member? Someone he was indebted to, maybe? Was he in any trouble?"

But neither Eve nor Susan could answer my questions. Not a single one.

"I'm embarrassed, actually," Susan said, rubbing the graying hairs at her temples. "I don't know anything about the man I'd see from week to week. Now I realize how private he was. He was gregarious and always good for a laugh or a broad compliment, but he didn't share much about his personal life. Or maybe I never took enough interest. Perhaps I should have asked him more about his life. He would talk for hours about recipes and ingredients, but he never divulged anything personal."

"It's not your fault," I reassured Susan. "Not everyone is forthcoming about their life." I paused. I'd been guilty of that myself. But then there was a lot about my life, and my powers, that I could never explain to strangers or even my best friend, Gina. Could Luca and I have had more in common than I thought? Was there something in his life that he wanted to keep quiet?

Eve finished her espresso and got up to polish glasses. "Luca would come in here some evenings, usually on our quieter nights, never weekends, and order the most elaborate dish on the menu, sometimes asking for adjustments, which drove Sol mad."

I smiled. I could totally imagine Sol wringing his hands in the kitchen when a customer asked to alter one of his carefully designed dinners.

"But still," she continued, "I never knew much about his life beyond his eating habits."

I sighed. It was so saddening to hear that neither Susan nor Eve really knew much about Luca. Still, this was a small village, and I was certain that if he'd had a girlfriend, Eve would have known. Wouldn't he have brought her to the inn for his special dinners that made Sol crazy?

I suppose it was because Luca had spoken to me on his way to the next realm, but I felt some responsibility, like it was up to me to shed light on the mystery of Luca's life.

Gerry pretended to lick one of the glasses Eve had just polished. I had to stop myself from laughing at his foolishness. I didn't want to encourage him. Suddenly, he leaned over and said, "Ask who else was in the foraging group. Stands to reason if someone killed him with mushrooms, they had to know their fungi too."

"Oh, good point," I said aloud. Gerry had his moments.

"Pardon?" Susan asked.

"Thinking aloud." Then I asked Susan who else was in

the foraging group while Gerry made an elaborate thumbs-up gesture.

"There's only eight of us," Susan said. "Sol and his brother. A young woman who works in the kitchen at Broomewode Hall; I can't remember her name. And Lauren just joined. Do you remember her?"

I nodded. How could I forget Lauren, my first (and incidentally only) wedding cake customer, whose fiancé died the night before the wedding? She'd struck up a friendship with Edward, who was now the gamekeeper at Broomewode Hall. I asked Susan if he was in the group, too.

"Yes," Susan replied. "They joined together. And then there's Tony, who works at the post office, and Melinda, the tailor."

I made a note of the names. These were seriously useful leads.

Susan trailed off. "I simply feel terrible. Why didn't I know more about Luca? Not only did I see him on foraging expeditions, Reg and I recently joined the Broomewode Choir, and we attended practice together."

"Oh!" I exclaimed. I'd almost forgotten that Eve had told me Susan was in the choir. Now I had two leads. "I know you're new to the choir, but did you witness any tension between any of the choir members and Luca? Any small spats or disagreements? Maybe something that might trigger murderous thoughts or actions?"

Susan snorted. "Poppy, it's a choir, for goodness' sake. Could you think of a purer reason for people to gather? Well, I say pure—Luca did flirt with all the women shamelessly. And he was a bit of a peacock. Said he'd been trained by the best opera singers in the world, which are in Italy, of course."

Aha. So Luca had been a trained singer. Was the woman who Florence saw with the music papers his instructor? That would certainly make sense. As did the idea of him being an outrageous flirt. From my brief encounters with Luca, it was like he had one setting: gregarious and smooth-tongued.

"Was there anyone in particular he flirted with?"

"He treated everyone the same way," Susan said. "That's how you knew he was harmless." She sipped her cappuccino thoughtfully. A little foam graced her top lip, and she artfully licked it away. "There was one woman he seemed to flirt with less than everyone else. In fact, I noticed it because he didn't talk to her at all during practice. But then last week I spied them whispering together by the side of the church. I don't know her name. I don't think we ever spoke to her. Soprano. Pretty voice."

I wondered if Luca had been hiding his real affection by blatantly flirting with all the other women in the choir, or the entire village, for that matter.

"Is her hair blond?" I asked, daring to get my hopes up.

But Susan shook her head. "No, she has dark hair."

Huh. Go figure. As if sleuthing were ever that easy.

I asked Susan when the choir met, and she told me every Saturday afternoon, which was excellent news for one amateur snoop.

"We're still having a rehearsal today, in spite of the death, so we can have a memorial for Luca in song. We'll do something more formal later, but this is a way for us to come together and honor him."

Eve leaned across the bar and squeezed Susan's hand.

I wondered whether to approach the foraging group first or the choir members. It was hard to know which route would lead me to answers. But before I could ask any more questions, Eve glanced at her watch. Reflexively, I did the same. Half an hour had passed, and while I'd been sipping coffee and languishing at the bar, Eve had downed her coffee, polished glasses, and now she was unpacking crates of wine. She really knew how to multitask.

"I know that faraway look," Eve admonished. "You're trying to piece together parts of the puzzle, but you're supposed to start making the cakes for the weekend, not do the police's work for them."

Sheepishly, I agreed. Any thoughts I might have entertained about taking off to Broomewode Knoll Church would have to wait. For now. I went to take my place in the kitchen.

CHAPTER 11

$\mathcal{T}$he kitchen was empty when I pushed through its swinging doors, and the sun cast the room in a gorgeous glow, the light bouncing off the steel surfaces and creating diagonal shadows across the polished floor. Through the window over the sink, I could see Sol and Pavel unloading a delivery of fresh and dry produce. I decided to leave them to it and get cracking with my cakes. The radio had been left on, and a country and western song played softly. It was familiar, and not knowing the words, I hummed the tune, trying to still my racing mind.

I had to make three cakes for the weekend: carrot with cream cheese frosting, coffee and walnut loaf, a classic Victoria sponge and, of course, the chocolate hazelnut torte. I was working from tried and tested recipes which (if I say so myself) I had mastered in the first stages of preparing the competition. "Basics first," my best friend Gina's dad, the baker, had advised, and he'd been right. I'd had to learn the ins and outs to making all the seemingly simple cakes, and by practicing these over and over, I'd given myself the foundations from which to build more exciting, adventurous cakes. And Gina agreed, after many sampling sessions, that I'd nailed the moist crumb these kinds of cakes needed. At the time, it was the highest praise I'd ever received, and I was on cloud nine.

After all that time in the tent trying to outdo myself with ambitious and innovative bakes that were briefly sampled by the judges and then passed on to the hungry crew, I was enjoying cooking for customers who didn't taste my cakes only to criticize.

After watching my muffins devoured by happy customers and seeing all the rhubarb Danish had been eaten, I knew now that the real joy of food was sharing it with others, not racing for a prize. Nerdy or not, it was exciting to me that now dozens of strangers would be sampling my cakes over the weekend, treating themselves to something sweet. Thankfully, I wasn't in charge of bread. That came from Sol's brother in the neighboring village.

I arranged my tools and ingredients on the work surface and opened up my recipe book and spreadsheets. I had to be very careful to get all the timings of the different cakes right, so I was working from an Excel sheet. A little over the top? Maybe. But I didn't want to mess up a single thing.

It was very different working in the Broomewode Inn kitchen than in the tent with the spotlights and with the intense pressure. It was nice to be more relaxed, but I couldn't help but wonder what was happening in the tent about now. The remaining contestants would be in the midst of their signature challenge. Would Maggie be wowing with her more innovative take on the classics this week, or would she find it a struggle? How were Florence's well-rehearsed lines for the cameras going down? Did she really charm the judges as much as she thought?

I was particularly worried about Hamish. Over the past two weeks, his self-confidence had taken a battering, and I knew from some pretty horrendous experience myself that baking nerves could lead to silly mistakes. Gaurav appeared to be the most calm, consistent baker, even though he was the shyest, or maybe just quietest, member of the group. Sometimes his flavor combinations could be a little off-piste. But I wondered if he might take the lead this week. What was it people said? That you had to watch out for the quiet ones? Maybe Gaurav's ambition was greater than anyone thought.

Standing in the empty kitchen, for a moment I suddenly felt very alone. I missed my friends and the excitement of the tent terribly. But then, of course, Gerry somersaulted in and suddenly all I longed for was peace.

"Pops!" he said, "I'm loving having you around the place more. Your new job is really working out for me. Before I was lonely, and you were so worried about the cameras following you around in the baking tent, but now, here we are, chatting freely. I can talk to you whenever I want."

How about whenever *I* wanted, huh? Or more exactly, *didn't* want.

"In fact," he continued, clearly on a roll, "apart from being able to float through walls, you getting booted out of the competition is the best thing that's happened to me since I became brown bread."

"Brown bread?" I glanced up, confused.

He rolled his ghost eyes. "Brown bread, dead. Cockney rhyming slang. I can see you need your American education broadened." Here he settled himself beside me on the counter top. "Don't fall down the apples and pears," he said.

I rolled my eyes. Everybody knew this one. "Stairs."

"Very good."

"I'm a bit short of the bees and honey," he said, as I got to mixing my cake batter.

"What?"

He rubbed his fingers against his thumb. Bees and honey? "Oh, money."

"Right."

"I like my meat with a bit of the army and navy."

I chuckled, starting to catch on. "Horseradish?" I teased.

"No, gravy. And here comes the bottle and stopper," Gerry said, his wide-eyed gaze staring behind me. I glanced around, hearing someone come in. Gerry whispered, "Bottle and stopper, copper."

Sure enough, Adam Lane walked in. "Poppy. Sorry to bother you at work."

"It's okay. What can I do for you?"

"I wanted to let you know that the spaghetti sauce in Luca's kitchen was, indeed, riddled with death caps. That's what killed him." He turned a worried eye on me. "Would have killed you, too, if you'd eaten it."

Frustration filled me. I was as certain as an intuitive water witch could be that Luca had been intentionally poisoned. "But chanterelles don't look anything like death caps," I said as though he might not know this.

"No. There were loads of chanterelles in the sauce too. The theory is that he was mixing mushrooms and mistook the death cap for another sort. I've forgotten the names, but we checked with an expert who said there are several mushrooms that can be mistaken for the death cap. Seems the Italian grocer got careless."

"So that's it?" I couldn't believe they were going to stop investigating.

Obviously hearing my surprise, he said, "The investigation is ongoing, of course, but sometimes people do die by accident, Poppy."

In my experience, not around here.

I tipped the batter from the mixer into pans.

He said, "Luca was popular. Had no alarming debts, no criminal record or associations. It seems very much like a tragic accident." Then he paused as though uncertain whether to continue. "I'm only glad you weren't poisoned. Or Florence."

"Me, too."

"Well, I'll be off. Do call me if you have any questions."

"Thanks. I will."

As he left, I thought for poor Luca's sake that I would have to take a hand in figuring out what had happened to the deli owner. Sure, I knew that his poisoning could have been accidental, but it could also have been set up to look like an accident.

Which was it?

Adam had barely left when Gerry made a rude noise. "Look at him in his fiddle and flute telling you old Luca died by accident."

"Fiddle and flute?" I was so confused.

"His suit. And if you ask me, that copper should make better use of his mince pies." He tapped his eyes to save me asking.

"I don't think Luca poisoned himself by accident, but it's

hard to explain to the police that I saw a wineglass that still looked damp turned the wrong way in Luca's cabinet or that the ghost of Luca spoke to me. The police will think I'm joyful and glad."

"What?"

I felt quite pleased with myself. "Joyful and glad. Mad."

"Pops, darling. You stick to baking. Leave the rhyming slang to the Cockneys, eh?"

"I have to do something, Gerry. What if a murderer goes free?"

"Well, that won't happen since you get to make use of my ghostly assistance."

"Really?" I slid the cake pans in the oven and wished them well.

Gerry snorted. "You know very well that being invisible to everyone but you is very helpful in sniffing out clues to all the mysterious goings-on in Broomewode."

I couldn't argue there. "Have you heard anyone talking about Luca?" I asked, hopeful that he might have overheard snatches of conversations that would give us some potential leads.

But he shook his head. "Not yet, but I'm all ears." He pulled at his slightly sticky-out ears, and I giggled. His red spiky hair was still standing at perfect points.

"You know," I said, pointing at his shirt patterned with trucks and cars, "if you were still alive, that shirt would stink so much, it would walk itself straight off your back and into the washing machine."

Gerry laughed. "I guess not having to do laundry is one upside to being a ghost."

"Maybe you could make yourself useful and do mine," I

said but abruptly stopped talking as Sol walked into the kitchen, staggering under the weight of a crate of tomatoes.

"You okay, Wilkinson?" he said, bemused. "Talking to yourself is the first sign of madness, you know." He set the tomatoes down on the worktop.

"Just singing along to the radio," I said before realizing that the local news was on.

I steeled myself for Sol to tease me further, but to my surprise, he burst into song instead.

"Brightest and best of the sons of the morning,
Dawn on our darkness and lend us Thine aid;
Star of the East, the horizon adorning,
Guide where our infant Redeemer is laid.

He had a lovely, strong tenor voice. Clear and bright. But my true excitement came from recognizing the song. I wasn't sure of the name, but I knew exactly where I'd heard it before.

He finished, and I applauded. "Wonderful!" I said. "I'd no idea you could sing."

"One of my favorites, that one. Brightest and best, Reginald Heber."

I knew it. A man singing a hymn in a kitchen probably meant...

"Are you part of the church choir?" I asked, hoping beyond hope that his answer would be *yes*.

"I am," he replied.

I stifled a great big grin. This was a tasty development.

"Me and the wife, Bobbi. It's intense fitting it in around my work schedule, but it's the one thing we do together. She's a hairdresser and often works long hours, sometimes into the night with private clients. Honestly, I don't know why people need a haircut at dinnertime, but there you go—that's the crazy modern world we live in."

I murmured some sounds that I hoped came across as sympathetic, but really, I was just waiting for an appropriate moment to dig a little deeper.

"I don't suppose Luca was in the choir with you?" I asked, pretending innocence in what I hoped was a casual voice.

At my question, Sol's face fell. "Aye, yes. He was. Poor chap. He was the best of all the male singers—had a voice we all envied, which, truth be told, I think he enjoyed. The envy, I mean."

I told Sol I'd heard Luca singing opera while he was foraging. I'd been really impressed.

"Sounds about right. He outsang us all. There was a bit of harmless jealousy in the group, as the choir conductor always gave him the solos."

Harmless jealously? Was there such a thing? I waited, hoping Sol would say more.

"Also," he said, bending over the crate of tomatoes and examining the produce with a critical eye, "Luca had this annoying habit of giving the other singers tips." He pushed the crate to one side, obviously satisfied with the fruits, and began to unpack it.

I picked up a wooden spoon and distractedly stirred my batter, making sure it was fully mixed. "Tips? How do you mean?"

Sol turned back to me and in a bad Italian accent said, "No, no, no. You must *feel* the music. Imagine you have a string pulling your head up, up, like a puppet. *Capisce?* And now open the mouth, that's it, and lift the palate. *Su!* Up!"

I giggled. Even though I felt bad that the guy was dead, Sol's impression of Luca was pretty bang on. He definitely had a way with mimicry. Luca did have a very melodic way of communicating, his voice lilting and always emphasizing certain words, bits of Italian breaking through into the English.

"But we won't speak ill of the dead," Sol said, collecting himself, suddenly all business. "And we won't be late with those cakes either," he added.

I gulped and whispered, "Nope." The last thing I wanted to do was irk my new boss. I reminded myself to stay on track, not lose my way following police investigations like I had with the competition. Eve was right. *Time to focus, Pops.*

CHAPTER 12

*G*erry disappeared, and Sol and Pavel worked on getting lunch ready and dinner prepped while I continued with the cakes. I finished all of my cakes on time, the ones for the afternoon and the ones for the evening dessert tray, and had them ready for service. I was proud of my bakes—they tasted and looked professional, but the best thing was that no one was about to stick them on a judging table. I wondered again how the other bakers were doing and looked forward to hearing about the day later this evening.

Once Sol was satisfied with my work, I could finally take off my flour-dusted apron and follow my lead about the choir. Sol told me the choir practiced at three o'clock for two hours, which left him time to get back in time for dinner.

I was done by two, which gave me time to drive home to my cottage and listen to Gateau's meows of discontent at being left alone overnight. I made a fuss of her and opened a can of her favorite gourmet cat food, which I put down next to her dry food that automatically refilled and the cat fountain that kept her in constant fresh water.

Mildred appeared in the kitchen and sniffed. "I suppose you've been off enjoying yourself, have you? Never a thought for us stuck here on our own?"

"Mildred," I asked her, "did you ever forage for mushrooms when you were alive?"

She turned up her nose. "Nasty damp toadstools that grow in the muck. Course not."

Right, no help there, then.

I indulged in a quick shower and changed into a jean skirt and sleeveless white blouse and grabbed a sweater in case it cooled off later. I slipped my feet into sandals and headed back to Broomewode once more.

It was a lovely afternoon, and what harm could really come from a stroll to Broomewode Knoll Church to hear some singing, I said to myself, trying to push any worry about my safety from my mind. Elspeth and Jonathon had freaked me out a bit. I touched my amethyst necklace and steeled myself against negative thoughts. I'd miss most of the practice-cum-memorial, but hopefully I'd get a sense of the group by watching them.

If the police weren't treating this as a suspicious death, then I had a duty to get them on the right track. Eve's warnings to stay out of it echoed in my ears, as did Elspeth's and Jonathon's, but surely there was nothing safer than a bunch of well-meaning choir members gathering to practice and pay their respects to their friend.

I parked outside the inn, thinking I'd walk over from there, but Eve came outside and asked where I was heading. I must have looked sheepish because she shook her head and then pointed to a beautiful red bicycle resting against the wall beside the delivery doors, a matching red helmet slung over its handlebars. I looked from Eve's smiling face to the bike and back again.

"If I know you, Poppy Wilkinson," Eve said, "and I think I do, you're off to snoop at the choir practice. But I don't have a good feeling about all this sleuthing. Since you aren't going to heed my warnings, then at least I can make you a little more mobile."

She walked over to the bike. "Poppy, meet Mavis, my bicycle. She's been with me for ten years, and she rides like a dream."

I immediately walked closer to the bike. "I had no idea you rode a bike to work." I had a sudden, wonderful image of Eve's long, gray braid flying out behind her as she pedaled across the village.

"She goes faster than she looks, so if you get into any trouble, you can zip away, you hear?"

I went over to the bike and ran my fingers along its smooth chrome. "Mavis, you're a beaut," I said.

I thanked Eve and told her not to worry. I'd take care of myself and Mavis.

"Take care, little sister. Blessed be."

"I promise," I said. "I'll keep my eyes and ears open for any signs of danger."

I settled Eve's helmet on my head and adjusted the chin strap, and then swung my leg over the saddle. I hadn't ridden a bike since I visited my parents in the South of France almost ten months ago, and I was giddy with excitement. I saluted Eve and told her I'd return the bike in an hour or so.

I felt a little wobbly at first, but my feet soon found the

groove of the pedals, and they pushed, pushed, pushed, heading for the road that would take me through the village and out the other side to the church.

Turning from the tarmac and onto the grass, I careered onwards, veering into the heart of the quiet, rustling peace of the village as Mavis's wheels rolled me over the terrain. I felt free in a way that my little car, as much as I loved it, didn't provide. It was the feeling of the wind in my face, the scents of the grass and flowers. I had a sense of being watched and looked up to see the hawk I'd come to think as connected to my father gliding high overhead like he was surfing the clouds. The sun was warm on my bare legs as I coasted forward, steering round the bends, grateful that the roads were almost empty of cars, until I saw the old stone church up ahead and pedaled faster, switching the gears back up to give myself some resistance.

Broomewode Knoll Church stood on a small rise above the village, set back from the aptly named Church Lane. It had an ancient stone border and a steep set of steps, over the top of which an arch of white roses grew. I dismounted, took off the helmet, and climbed the stairs, setting Eve's bike down by a blooming blue hydrangea bush. A small graveyard sat on the left side of the church, its old headstones crumbling and sinking at angles into the earth. A few of the headstones were more recent, including the large memorial to the previous viscount who'd died so young. The scene should have been peaceful, but it wasn't. As hard as I tried, I couldn't shake off the weird feeling that nothing was as it seemed in this village. I reminded myself that Susan would be at the practice and Reg and Sol, too. It was the middle of a sunny afternoon, and I was about to enter a church. My fears were absurd.

I approached an elaborate doorway, which I'd read in one of the local brochures was constructed in Norman times. The rest of the church was built much later, so the brochure had said, with a tall perpendicular tower and early 14th-century south porch and south transept. A single daisy was growing out of the path as I grew closer.

I could hear the singing from outside and wondered if I'd be able to sneak in unnoticed so that I could get a good look at the choir without drawing attention to myself. Well, there was only one way to find out.

The door to the church was ajar, probably to let in some fresh air, and I slid my body through the small gap. Inside, I had to hold in a gasp as I took in my surroundings. The church interior was lovely. The arch-shaped stained-glass windows let in multicolored light that patterned the stone flooring and rows of pews. The pews themselves were intricately carved with their own swirling patterns, which on closer inspection were leaves and vines. On the walls hung a series of intriguing carvings, all of which involved animals. One tableau showed a tale of a fox and geese, another a pelican with her head bent towards her breast. A third depicted a hawk in mid-flight, and my heart beat double quick. Was this a sign that I was in the right place?

The carvings brought back a sudden memory of my dad from when we lived in the Pacific Northwest. He loved to go antique hunting, trawling the shops and markets. He had the patience to sit all day on a folded chair in a hot auction tent, flapping himself with the brochure, waiting for the lot he had his eye on. I never understood it, but he liked the ones almost beyond repair, the ones that everyone else would overlook, and he'd buy them for a fistful of dollars and spend weekends in his woodwork shed restoring them to their former glory. I gently touched the carving of the hawk and felt connected to my birth dad and the wonderful man who raised me.

But I couldn't allow myself to be distracted. The choir was gathered in a semicircle at the far end of the church, just behind a simple but beautifully designed pulpit. I edged closer, determined to study the group as they sang. I didn't recognize the hymn, but it had a melancholy air—a feeling of longing and loss. As I tiptoed along the side of the church, I passed a large memorial to John de Champnee, which showed the carved figure in three-quarter relief, set into an oval niche. No doubt this was an ancestor of the current Champneys.

The choir's singing rose and fell in accordance with the choirmaster's sweeping hands, and I stopped, caught in the harmony of their song.

The verse died away, and one voice began to sing. It was Sol. His deep tenor echoed through the building, and I slipped into a pew unnoticed and listened.

The choirmaster clasped his hands together, and the rest of the singers turned to one another, smiling.

"Lovely, Sol. Luca must be smiling down at you," the choirmaster began. I squinted, trying to get a better look at his face. He seemed to be in his sixties, with salt and pepper hair neatly parted to one side. He was wearing square black glasses and a checked shirt. I couldn't recall if I'd ever seen him at the inn.

"I know we've all been saddened by the news of his untimely death this morning," he continued. "I believe that Luca can feel the vibrations of our love and affection from his place in heaven."

There were murmurs of agreement from the group. I spotted Susan and Reg immediately. Sol and the younger man I guessed was his brother stood beside them, and then there was the woman who must have been Sol's wife, Bobbi. She wasn't exactly what I'd pictured as the woman who matched Sol, with his bulldog face and tattoos. She was more glamorous than I'd imagined, with blond hair cut in a fashionable blunt bob that swung around her neck, big gold hoop earrings, and a face painted so carefully, Gina would be proud. Or would she? Gina always thought "less was more" when it came to makeup, and Bobbi certainly erred on the "more" side. Her lips were glossy and caught the light. And her clothes, too, seemed incongruous with our surroundings: tight white pedal pushers and heeled sandals. Next to Sol and his brother, she looked tiny.

"But one thing that I know Luca would want is for the show to go on, which brings us to the sad business of giving his solos to new singers."

At this, the group stood to attention, and all turned to face the choirmaster. I took in the other faces. There was my kitchen friend, Belinda, from Broomewode Hall and next to her a woman I'd never seen before. She was wearing a black shirtdress with pearl buttons, her dark brown hair in loose waves around her shoulders. Next to her was a meek-looking man with a sloping forehead and downturned mouth, in his late thirties, perhaps.

While I was studying the group, the choirmaster assigned Sol one of Luca's solos. His brother high-fived him, which I thought was a little crass. His wife gave him a kiss on the cheek, and as she leaned over him, I noticed a heart tattoo on her right shoulder. "And the other solo will go to Logan."

The meek-looking man beamed and looked longingly over at the woman in the black dress, trying to catch her eye. She was staring off into the distance, her attention trained on the enormous stained-glass windows. She was a little younger than the man who so clearly adored her and would have been pretty if it weren't for the lost expression on her face, her pale skin indicative of loss of sleep rather than her natural skin tone. She seemed distracted. I wondered if this was the woman that Susan told me Luca had been talking with so intimately last week.

The practice was coming to an end, and a little spying done, I stood and made my way over to Susan and Reg.

Reg smiled broadly as he saw me approach and beckoned me over with a wave of his bear-like hands. He was standing next to the choirmaster, who turned in surprise, obviously not realizing he'd had an audience.

"Poppy," Reg said, "how lovely to see you. Susan didn't say you were coming down."

I blushed a little. What could I say? I didn't tell Susan so that I could spy on you all, because I knew she'd be worried that I was getting mixed up in yet another police investigation?

But Reg didn't wait for an explanation. Instead, he introduced me to the choirmaster, whose name was Hugo.

"A pleasure to meet you, Poppy," he said. "Are you an aspiring singer?"

I had a voice like a ferry horn and told him so. "Honestly, I wouldn't wish the sound of my singing on my worst enemy."

At this, Hugo looked a little puzzled as to why I was there. Luckily, Susan jumped in. "Poppy was a friend of Luca's," she said quietly. "I told her we were dedicating today's choir practice in his memory."

"Ah," Hugo said, "Luca was a friend to us all. A warm, bubbling personality whose enthusiasm for life affected everyone he met. In fact, that reminds me."

Hugo turned to the rest of the choir, who were chatting in groups. "Remember that we're heading over to Broomewode Inn now to celebrate Luca's life. Everyone is welcome."

Hugo turned back to me. "That includes you, too, Poppy. Let me gather the troops and we'll talk more later." But Hugo walked away before I could reply, and Reg went with him.

Susan raised her eyebrows at me. "I thought you were supposed to be staying away from snooping, but I suppose I should be used to your headstrong ways by now. You're just like my precious Sly, in fact. Stubborn to the core but with the biggest heart."

I gave Susan my best bashful *Well, you know me* face.

Susan raised a brow at me like I was a wayward child. "Since you're here now—" She made a small gesture across the room. "That's the one I think Luca was holding a candle for."

I followed her gaze to the woman with the dark brown hair. I was right. I asked if she'd be going to the pub, and Susan nodded. "Be careful though, Poppy, whatever you're planning. Emotions are raw at the moment."

I looked around at the rest of the choir, who were talking loudly and joking around as they packed up their things. Were emotions really that raw? Sol and the other man who'd been assigned solos seemed particularly bright.

"Are they?" I said to Susan. "Everyone appears very chipper."

"Remember, Poppy, things aren't always what they seem on the surface."

She had a point.

I waited as the choir got themselves together. Sol introduced me to his wife. "Poppy's our new cake and pastry chef."

She nodded as though she didn't much care whether I made cakes or changed spark plugs for a living. Up close, she was even more carefully made up than I'd thought. It was hard to get a read on her. She didn't seem too interested in meeting me. "That's nice," she said.

We walked out into the glorious sunshine, and I collected Eve's bike from the hydrangea bush.

The woman Susan pointed out to me walked ahead of the others, and I caught up with her, determined to find out if she'd been closer to Luca than anyone knew.

I introduced myself and told her how sorry I was to hear about Luca's death.

She looked at me a little blankly and then offered a small smile, whispering, "Thank you." Up close, I noticed that she had pretty green eyes and a smattering of freckles across her nose. She wore a silver bracelet, and heart-shaped silver studs decorated her lobes.

"Did you know Luca well?" I asked, hoping it sounded casual, as I struggled to keep her pace with Mavis at my side.

"We sang in the choir together," she said, letting the sentence hang in the air, as if that answered my question.

"And have you been in the choir for a long time?"

"A while," she said.

She didn't even look at me as we spoke, just stared at the road ahead. She was obviously upset, and I felt bad for probing her at such a delicate time, but if the mystery of

106

Luca's death was going to be solved, then I needed all the information I could get. I was thinking of ways to reframe the same question when the guy who'd been staring at her during practice slid next to the two of us. Great.

"Sorry to interrupt, Vera, but Hugo wants to know if you could bring the new song sheets next week."

So this was Vera. I'd finally found her. This was the woman whose name Luca spoke as his dying words. He'd wanted her to know he was sorry.

Naturally, I wondered what he was sorry for and if it had anything to do with his death.

CHAPTER 13

To my frustration, Vera quickly excused herself from our conversation and slipped away to talk to Hugo. I was left with the eager and obviously lovelorn man who introduced himself as Logan. Once he'd discovered I was a baker, he began telling me all about his prizewinning scones. He'd won a prize for them at the village fete two years ago. Honestly, was I ever going to escape Broomewode's obsession with the wretched scone?

I tried to find some inner Zen as I listened to him prattle on about sultanas versus currants, but my mind couldn't help but wander back to Vera. Why had she implied that she and Luca weren't close if she was the last person he was thinking of before he passed to the other side? What was she hiding? And why?

Vera struck me as someone who was quiet and thoughtful, though that could have been simply because she was grieving. Of all of the choir members, she and Hugo seemed the most saddened by Luca's death.

Back at the inn, I returned Eve's bike and helmet to where

she'd parked and thought hard about what my next move would be with the choir. I had to get to the bottom of the group dynamics without drawing too much attention to myself. I could use Sol and Susan as buffers, of course, explaining away my interest in the choir as that of a well-meaning friend and colleague.

The pub was already crowded, and as I entered, I was presented with a dilemma. At the bar, Susan, Reg, and Logan had arrived ahead of the others; at our usual table were the bakers. I stood, looking from one to other, paralyzed as to where to go first.

The bakers looked exhausted but happy, a feeling I knew oh too well. They were talking loudly, caught up in that post-bake rush. It was weird—I wanted to join them, hear all about the day, but as I wasn't in the running any longer, it also was sort of none of my business. I shouldn't expect to be privy to the ins and outs of the competition simply because I was a past contestant. But they were my friends, too, and I cared about them deeply. While I stood dithering, Hamish spotted me, and just like that, the decision was taken out of my hands.

"Poppy, come and join us," Hamish belted in his broad Scottish voice. The other bakers looked up and waved me over, and I went, eager to hear their news.

They were opening a bottle of red wine, and Gaurav passed me a glass as though I were still one of them.

The bakers were all talking at once. From what I could gather, Jonathon had been particularly harsh today and had doled out the criticism as smoothly as spreading perfect buttercream.

"When he criticized the tartness of my lemons, I simply thought I was going to die," Florence wailed.

"Och, he had nothing good to say to anyone," Hamish commiserated.

"He sucks," Gaurav agreed.

"I'm sure he's only trying to add excitement for the home viewer," I suggested.

Four furious faces turned to me.

I raised my hands in defense. "Okay, okay, he sucks!" I laughed.

"Indeed," Maggie said. "He *sucks lemons.*"

We laughed, and any sorrow I felt at not being in the tent today disappeared. The last thing I wanted was to deal with Jonathon's sharp tongue and sharper criticism. I'd said the words idly, but suddenly, I thought they might be true. Jonathon was almost practiced in his harsh comments. I recalled him memorizing his own recipes and wondered if he also memorized lines he could say in front of the camera about the contestants' efforts. After all, he and Elspeth knew ahead of time what everyone was planning.

From the garbled chatter, I discerned that Gaurav had come first in the signature bake, Florence second, Maggie third, and Hamish last. But Hamish had turned it around in the technical, coming in on top, with Maggie at the bottom and Florence just scraping third place. I wondered if Florence secretly blamed me for her struggle today. She'd been pretty annoyed that Adam Lane had questioned her last night when she needed her sleep. But if she'd stuck around at Luca's like she should have, maybe Florence would have gotten to sleep a little earlier. I was also surprised that Maggie had been last in the technical. Had she lost her nerve after baking outside her comfort zone?

Of course, I wasn't the only one missing out on the competition action. Gerry soon floated over from goodness knows where he'd been lurking and hovered over the seat next to Florence. He crossed his legs, genie style. "What's the goss, Pops?" he asked. "Whose lemon curd is sinking to the bottom of the sponge? Whose meringues are looking a bit peaky?"

"What was the technical challenge?" I asked, doing my best to ignore Gerry's somersaults.

"Tiramisu," the bakers replied in unison.

"Nightmare," Hamish said.

"Dreadful," Maggie added.

"Exhausting," Gaurav said.

I looked at Florence, amazed. She was pale and downcast. "Shameful," she whispered. "Can you imagine what the world is going to say about me and my proud Italian heritage? I've been making tiramisu with my nona since I was seven years old. I know the very best way to soak the sponges so they drink up the coffee and brandy. I know exactly how to whisk the eggs to get the mix frothy and light but still stiff enough to hold. I know how to create delicate, wafer-thin layers so that the whole thing looks glamorous, not an oozing mess. And yet..."

She hung her head. I was genuinely baffled. How *had* Florence messed this up? It was literally *her thing.* She was so proud of her Italian heritage; she should have won that challenge in her sleep.

Maggie reached across the table and patted Florence's

arm. "Sometimes it's the things we know the best that mess us up. We don't apply the same concentration."

"Yeah," said Gerry, animated all of a sudden, "like how most car accidents happen a few meters from your home because people pay less attention to surroundings they know well."

Thanks for that, Gerry. I set down my wine, remembering that I would be driving back to my cottage tonight.

There was silence for a moment as Florence gathered herself together.

"Well, it just means that I'll have to pull it out of the bag tomorrow with my showstopper," she said finally, flicking her ponytail over one shoulder.

"Tell me everything," I said to the whole group. "I can't wait to hear what you've all concocted. I was making cakes this morning, feeling so grateful they weren't complicated and wouldn't be judged, but now I can live vicariously through you."

Maggie shot me a sympathetic look, but I just smiled. I meant it. Listening to the bakers talk, I realized I really didn't miss the tension of the tent. Working under that kind of duress was exhausting, worrying about the cameras, worrying about dropping a finished cake on the floor, forgetting an ingredient, forgetting more than one ingredient, forgetting the recipe, saying the wrong thing to Jilly and Arty, being judged harshly by Elspeth and Jonathon... Argh, the list went on. Nope. I was doing just fine without all that, thank you very much.

But I was invested in the competition. And I was genuinely interested in the more technical side of things. Between them, the remaining contestants were so inventive.

Each of them had a different way of thinking about the same ingredients. Their backgrounds and experiences informed how they approached the same kind of recipe, and I loved how their personalities shone through. Although I was no longer part of the competition, I could still learn a lot from my baking friends.

The only thing I envied was their concentration. When you're inside the tent, everything else stays outside. Personal hardships and global dilemmas, all of that becomes white noise. It's just you and the whisk in sync, working through a recipe step by step. And every so often, if you need a hand or something isn't quite working, one of the other contestants will turn to you and offer a kind word or a bit of help. It was those moments I missed, the camaraderie, the neighborly familiarity.

Even though we were pitted against each other, the moment someone was in distress, the others would stop what they were doing and try to help. I remembered the other contestants who'd left before me: Amara, Priscilla, Evie, Daniel, Ewan—even awful Marcus, who disappeared after the first show. Each of them had taught me something, whether it was about baking or something more personal. Even Gerry had given me a gift of a sort, helping me solve some of the strange things that had happened here.

I snapped back to attention, realizing Hamish was explaining the showstopper challenge for tomorrow. "We have to include at least three layers. One needs to be a baked element of our choosing, another a set custard or mousse, and finally a jelly. A jelly! Can you believe they'd do that to us? Until this week, I hadn't eaten jelly since I was a wee boy. Even then I wasn't a big fan. All that wobbling."

"Don't forget it has to be sliceable," Gaurav added, putting his head in his hands. "Every time I've practiced my showstopper, the thing falls apart the second I take a knife to it. There's too much going on."

I listened agog as the bakers explained their multi-layered desserts. There were raspberry Swiss rolls, strawberry Eton Mess mousse, lemon panna cotta, and elderflower jelly. Strawberry mousse with prosecco, blueberry muffin sponge, coconut sponge, mini meringues, pineapple and mango jelly with floating white chocolate stars, yuzu curd, lemon curd, chili chocolate mousse, Portuguese custard layers flavored with cardamom and cinnamon, golden syrup sponge with butterscotch custard, caramel popcorn crunch bites. I couldn't keep up with the ideas as the group poured forth their most adventurous combinations yet.

"I don't know about you," Gerry said, "but my appetite—if I had one, of course—is certainly not stimulated by these desserts."

I rolled my eyes in his direction, and as I did, caught sight of Sol, strolling into the pub. He said something to Eve at the bar before heading straight for the kitchen. I felt for Sol—he worked such long hours, and after a full day and a choir practice, now he had to get himself geared up for dinner service.

As I listened to Gaurav talk about set custard, I kept my eye on the rest of the choir members as they arrived, mostly in pairs. They formed an awkward clump around the bar, and I wondered whether, outside the choir, these people had anything in common. They certainly didn't look like a group of friends. Bobbi, Sol's wife, walked in with the choirmaster. They were in deep discussion.

A sharp elbow nudged me in the ribcage, and I was about

to tell Gerry off when I remembered he couldn't poke. I turned, surprised. It was Florence.

"That's the woman I saw going to Luca's house. With the papers with the music notes on them."

I looked at Florence, confused. "Are you sure?"

"Yes, I'm sure. She was carrying a Dionigi purse when I saw her, and there it is again." She pointed at Bobbi's little red handbag. It had a long strap and a black and gold disc at the center. Bobbi held it to her body protectively, playing with the strap. "I remember looking at it because I happen to know that the particular design was only released in Italy, and I wondered whether she was loaded and had traveled to buy it or was it just a fake? Now I can see closer—it's definitely fake. You can tell by the positioning of the clasp. It's not central."

"Florence, your eye for fashion has paid off big time," I said, excusing myself from the table. "Back in a min."

I gave Gerry my best *Come with me* eyes, and he floated over to the bar. Bobbi had left the choirmaster's side and was heading into the kitchen. "Can you follow her?" I asked Gerry in a whisper. "I want to know what she and Sol talk about."

Gerry straightened and saluted me. "I'm on it, Pops!"

CHAPTER 14

I caught Eve's gaze at the bar, and she shot me an inquiring look. Philly, the new young barmaid, joined her, looking frantic. I could see she was desperate to ask Eve a question, but I was busy keeping her boss distracted by trying to communicate with eye contact alone. I wanted her to know that I thought I was onto something and that I'd put Gerry on the case without, you know, looking like I had something in my eye. If only telepathy was one of my powers, it would be *so* useful about now.

But Eve's attention was drawn back to serving as Philly tugged at her sleeve like a toddler and pointed at the choir members. They seemed to be asking for all kinds of different drinks. I excused myself from the baking group and hovered around the bar, doing my best to eavesdrop without drawing attention to myself.

It was Vera I was most interested in observing. She seemed disconnected, somehow, from the rest of the group, even though she was standing with the others. There was something faraway about her expression and demeanor. Like she was present in body but not in spirit. As the others talked excitedly about an upcoming performance, I saw that she turned her body slightly from the rest of the group and her eyes settled on a newspaper left at the edge of the bar.

She reached out and slid the paper towards her and then idly flicked through its pages. Her long, dark brown hair slid forward and blocked my view of her face. How I wished I could make out her expression. As she continued to turn over the pages, I noticed that she had long, slim fingers, musician's hands, and her nails were filed into perfect ovals. The cuticles were neat and pushed down, the nail a healthy pink and painted over with a shiny topcoat. No wedding ring.

Lovestruck Logan interrupted Vera's mindless page-turning and offered to buy her a drink. She shook her head and declined politely, but Logan waved Eve over anyway. "A red for me and a rosé for the lovely lady."

Eve smiled her professional smile—the one which was wider and toothier than her natural smile—and I watched as she twisted open the two bottles and poured a generous serving into each glass. Logan paid, Vera whispered a soft thank-you, and the two clinked glasses.

"To Luca," Logan said gallantly. But at that, Vera's eyes filled with tears. Logan looked horrified. "I'm sorry. I didn't mean to upset you, Vera. Just trying to toast the man's memory and all."

Vera swallowed, doing obvious battle with her emotions. I was about to intervene when Susan stood from the corner of the bar and ushered Vera to a table away from the crowd. Oh, lovely Susan, she always knew how to make someone feel better. She was so good at soothing a troubled soul, knew just the right words to say. It was a gift I envied. I always ended up rushing in like a bulldozer only to find myself speaking in platitudes or mortifying the poor person I was trying to console. But Susan was tender, thoughtful, full of wisdom. She had known loss herself, suffering through the untimely death of her husband. I gave them a moment to talk and looked away as Vera's tears spilled over and Susan nodded and listened.

I asked Eve for a tonic water and tried to stop my thoughts from racing. What was Vera and Luca's connection? Why was he so sorry? Had he hurt her? Misled her? Or was it something worse?

As was her way, Susan soon had Vera smiling again. I decided now was an appropriate time to join them. I couldn't get away from the fact that the last words Luca spoke were to tell Vera *I'm sorry*. She obviously cared for him deeply, and I knew how much it would mean for her to know she was his dying thought. But how could I honor Luca's last wish and give her the message without revealing that he spoke to me as ghost? Conundrum or what?

And that's when I had a brainwave. Finally!

I gestured to Eve and quickly whispered my plan. She should go over to Vera's table with her tarot cards and tell the poor woman that a reading would cheer her up. She was not to take no for an answer, and whatever the reading, Eve should "interpret" that Luca was sending her a message. He wanted her to know he was sorry.

Eve frowned. "I know it's important to get the message to Vera, but I can't use the cards for my own purpose. It doesn't work like that. The cards will reveal themselves."

Hmmm. She had a point. And Eve was a woman of integrity. I told Eve that I understood. The cards in her hands would surely lead Vera in the right direction, and if somehow the message was given at the same time, well then, two birds with one stone.

Eve seemed to soften. "You're right, the cards will do what the cards will do, and if I can slip Luca's last wish in there, then all the better."

She turned to Philly and asked her to hold the fort. The poor girl turned as pale as Gerry, but Eve reassured her she'd be fine. "You have to start learning to do things by yourself, luvvie," she said, and then slipped into the storeroom to get her cards.

As I waited, I felt something lifting from me. Eve would be able to pass on the message and I would have done my duty. Until this moment, I hadn't realized how heavy the burden of passing on someone's last wish really was.

Eve came out from the storeroom, and together we approached Susan and Vera. They were sitting in companionable silence, Susan holding Vera's hands as Vera's tear-stained face stared out of the window.

Eve asked if we could join them. "I've got just the thing for these troubled times." She set the cards on the table. "The tarot tells us stories about our lives and helps us make decisions about how to live them better. When I'm sad or at a crossroads, I always turn to the cards. It could help."

Susan looked at Vera, who turned away from the window and looked at us briefly and then shrugged. Eve took that as an invitation and pulled up the seat opposite. I sat next to Susan, who gave me a knowing look. Had Susan guessed my plan?

"My dear," Eve began, "all you have to do is concentrate on the cards."

Vera nodded.

Eve began to shuffle the deck. I started to feel nervous, hoping this would work. I shot a look over at the bakers' table, but they were deep in conversation. I hoped they stayed that way and Florence didn't barge in to the reading. I didn't think Vera needed to know that Florence had fled the scene of Luca's death.

"You must think of a question that you'd like to ask the cards and then I'll pull one card from the deck. Just don't tell me the question. Keep that to yourself. You'll pull three cards: one for the current situation, one for the course of action to be taken, and one for the result."

Vera couldn't have looked less interested if she'd tried. But still, she wasn't rude, and after letting her hand hover over the cards for a moment, she gently laid a finger on one, then another and finally, a third.

"Now remember that the cards are a practical guide to help you create your own future," Eve said, lowering her voice. "You are in control. The cards work with whatever energy you bring, and whatever your current circumstances, the gears of the future can always be changed. Tarot is about intuition, learning to listen."

Vera nodded.

I realized I was holding my breath and let it out slowly.

Eve turned over the first card. "The Fool. The Fool is a wanderer with a great enthusiasm for life, but he can be naïve, too. He gets himself into trouble and must learn from his mistakes." I couldn't help but think of Luca.

She turned over the second card.

"Ah, The Eight of Cups."

The image on the card was strange: the silhouette of a

man with his back to eight cups standing in the foreground. The cups were arranged in such a way that it looked like one was missing. Behind the man were mountains and a section of winding river. The moon in the night's sky illuminated a path ahead.

"What does it mean?" Vera asked quietly.

"This is an interesting card," Eve began. "The upright Eight of Cups appears as a helping guide to those unsure about fresh starts or new beginnings. For those in difficult situations, this card is perfect. It represents the wisdom and bravery when walking away from a situation. A fresh start is a tough choice to make, but a person is making it for a reason, and once you go forward, you cannot go back to your old life."

I couldn't take my eyes off Vera's face. It had transformed from melancholy to rapt. Clearly Eve had touched a nerve. I knew I could trust my coven sister to help.

Vera leaned forward and placed her delicate hands on the table. She touched the tarot card lightly, gently, as if it were a child or small animal.

"This card is about emotional courage, Vera. You might be feeling exhausted or weary, but you must take the path"—she tapped at the card—"*away* from the past."

Vera opened her mouth and then closed it again before saying, "The card really says all that?"

"It does," Eve said softly. "It's trying to show you the way."

She turned over the third card, and we all stared down, enthralled. "The Ten of Swords," Eve said.

The image was awful: a man lying down, ten swords plunged into his back. "This card is about recuperating, recovering after something traumatic. There are stars in that dark sky. Things look bleak now, but there is light ahead."

I looked at Eve, and she nodded. "I can feel a message in the cards, Vera. I think there's a person from your past who wants you to know they're sorry. I can feel regret. But it's time to be set free from all of that. I think this person wants you to be free to move on."

I held my breath again and watched Vera's face, expecting to see a rush of relief. But instead, she burst into tears.

"My dear, what's wrong?" Eve asked, alarmed.

Vera wailed even louder. "It's my fault! It's my fault that Luca is dead."

CHAPTER 15

*V*era collapsed into even greater sobs and put her head on the table. I looked at Susan and Eve, horrified. Did Vera just admit to murder?

"Whatever do you mean?" Susan asked softly, placing a hand on Vera's quaking back.

But Vera continued to cry, her whole body shaking.

"Did something happen you're not telling us?" Susan persisted.

Eve, usually so unflappable, looked seriously alarmed. This was not how the reading was supposed to go. The idea was to bring Vera some peace, not chaos. Eve was used to soothing souls, and she looked so uncomfortable, I felt terrible.

Philly called meekly from the bar that she needed help. *Great timing, Philly. Great timing.*

"Don't worry. I'll stay with her," Susan said to Eve. "Go— Poppy and I can take care of this."

But could we? I wished I had Susan's confidence. I was in the center of a seriously confusing situation. Vera was blaming herself for Luca's death. But then why would he want to say he was sorry? Had he brought the trouble on himself? I looked at The Fool card staring up at me. Luca might have played the fool. But then, when matters of the heart were involved, people often made fools of themselves.

Susan continued trying to calm Vera down, but nothing she said got through.

"If only I had my herbs," Susan whispered to me. "I could make her a soothing tonic."

I was about to say I could do with one of those myself when I saw Gerry floating over. As much as a ghost could, he looked paler than when he'd gone into the kitchen. I raised my brows.

"Woo-ee," he said, letting out a low whistle. "Some serious domestic drama is going down in there, dangerously close to a whole load of kitchen knives, I might add."

I glanced down again, this time at the tarot figure, prostrate with ten knives in his back.

I raised my eyebrows to Gerry. It was all I could do. The ghost always did this when he knew I couldn't talk back to him. I squinted at him, as if to say, *And? Spit it out!*

"Chef's wife just accused her husband of murdering Luca!"

I inhaled sharply. Vera continued to cry on the table. Susan looked up. "Is there...?"

I nodded and turned back to Gerry, signaling him to continue.

"And then Chef turned around and accused *her* of the crime. Said Luca had died by Bobbi's hand."

I was having trouble not yelling at Gerry. What was going on? Too many people were admitting to murdering Luca or accusing someone else. And this was a case the police deemed an accidental death.

Sol was gruff, for sure, and a little domineering, but over the last week, I'd seen how kind and patient he was underneath it all. He was dedicated to the inn and providing only the best quality food for the people of Broomewode. What would cause him to murder a fellow food aficionado? And then why would he accuse his own wife of murder? What possible reason would she have for killing Luca? Some choir disagreement? And here was Vera still sobbing, claiming she'd caused the death. It didn't make sense.

"Poppy?" Susan said. I stared back at her wild-eyed, wanting to spill what Gerry had just reported but knowing I'd have to wait until we were in private.

She'd been rubbing Vera's back in circles, and it must have done the trick because her sobs began to subside. She took a series of long breaths, and Susan and I watched, waiting for her final exhalation. She raised her head and looked at us forlornly.

"Luca invited me to dinner last night, you see, and I refused." Tears began to cascade down her face again.

So Florence and I hadn't been his first choice of dining companions then.

"Maybe if I'd gone, he'd still be alive. I could have saved him," Vera cried.

"Oh, my dear," Susan intoned. "Who knows? If you'd gone last night, then maybe—" She didn't finish the sentence but tapped her finger on the card of the person facedown with knives sticking out of their back.

"Why did you refuse his dinner invitation?" I asked.

Vera's tears flowed again, and Susan took out another

hankie and passed it to her. She dabbed at her eyes but still didn't answer my question. I felt for Vera, but she was so not helping a sister solve a murder right now.

"Did he act inappropriately toward you?" I asked. "Is that why you refused?"

At that, she just cried harder. "No, not at all," she said through her tears. "He was always the perfect gentleman."

I looked at Susan, baffled. None of this was making sense. Were Luca and Vera romantically involved? If so, why wouldn't she accept his dinner invitation? Had they fallen out? A lovers' tiff? Could that be the reason she was so upset?

I was about to probe further when Lovestruck Logan bumbled over. Once again, he was "sorry to interrupt" but asked Vera if she'd return to the group while they exchanged stories about Luca and raised a glass. "A wake of sorts," he said. "To honor our friend."

Vera agreed and stood, thanking Susan for her comfort and to us both for listening. She passed Susan back a soggy cotton hankie.

I watched as Logan awkwardly put an arm round Vera and guided her back to the group. The chef's wife, Bobbi, was with them. I studied her face. There was absolutely no sign that she'd had a nasty argument with her husband. She wasn't fidgeting or pacing, red-faced or fuming. Instead, she looked cool and collected. And in turn, I was suspicious.

I quickly filled Susan in on Gerry's kitchen sleuthing. He was proving to be extremely helpful today.

"They accused each other?" Susan asked, shaking her head.

"I know, right?"

"Better warn your friend. She's looking very cozy with a potential murderer right now." Susan pointed at the bar.

"Oh man," I groaned. It was Florence. She'd obviously gone to the bar to order some drinks but was now embroiled in a conversation with Bobbi, who was holding up the handbag Florence had told me was fake. I so hoped that wasn't what she was saying to Bobbi's face right now. Bobbi seemed so sassy and groomed, there was no way she'd take any kind of criticism about her appearance lightly. Especially not after a huge fight with her husband where they both accused each other of murder.

I approached the bar just as Florence was insisting that the Dionigi handbag was a limited edition only available in Italy. Florence's tone was soft as butter, but I knew her well enough to detect the edge of malice.

Bobbi was clutching the purse to her body defensively.

"It's just that I know the designer very well," Florence was saying. "Their goods are produced in the part of Italy where my family is from—they've been there for generations."

I sighed a little. It was always about Florence with Florence.

Bobbi straightened up, deciding not to be intimidated by my friend's gorgeous looks and her know-it-all fashion. "I bought it in a little boutique in Milan." She looked red in the face and very uncomfortable.

Nice save, Bobbi. But was it true?

I was about to interrupt when Edward came in, looking very country squire in his gamekeeper uniform. I'd been wanting to talk to Edward all week, but he'd been away on some estate business. I was hoping that he might have some information on the old gamekeeper, Mitty. If he was feeling better, I wanted to pay him a visit and ask him about local history, including my parentage. And then I was torn. Catch Bobbi in a moment of weakness and hope that she'd speak with me? Or ask Edward about the old gamekeeper, Mitty? I didn't want a murder investigation to sidetrack the search for my parents again.

I figured that since I'd passed on Luca's message, Bobbi (and Luca) could wait for a moment.

I walked to the other side of the bar and greeted Edward. He smelled of the outdoors, fresh air and cut grass. We chatted about the week, and I told him I'd gone to see the choir practice this afternoon and noticed Lauren wasn't there. He explained that she was sick with a summer cold and had spent the last two days in bed. Edward had made her his special chicken soup, and she was doing much better.

"I took some to Mitty, as well," Edward continued. "Honestly, I should can my recipe and sell it in stores—everyone I feed it to perks up immediately."

Wonderful. Edward had led the conversation exactly where I was trying to steer it.

"How's he doing?" I asked in as casual a voice as I could muster.

"Recovering nicely. Katie Donegal looks after him in her cottage. That woman has the energy of a sixteen-year-old. She loves to fuss over him and bring him sugary treats he's really not supposed to eat. But, as she says, a little of something naughty is nice."

"And his speech therapy?" I asked. If Mitty was talking, then I could visit him and see if he could answer some of the questions hanging in the air about my parents.

"He's getting his words back. It's slow progress, of course, but with Katie around, Mitty daren't give up. She's quite the taskmaster."

I smiled. That was exactly the kind of good news I needed to hear right now.

He grimaced and said Lauren had told him about Luca.

"I don't suppose she ever mentioned Luca being a flirt?" Edward laughed. "She didn't need to. I mean, Luca flirted with everyone. He flirted with me! He was that kind of character, you know? Larger than life. Broomewode won't be the same without him."

He went to the bar for a drink, and I decided to see if I could talk to Bobbi. Maybe the drink would have loosened her tongue. But as I turned to head over to the other side of the bar, I realized Bobbi had disappeared from the group.

"She went home," Susan whispered when I asked where she'd gone. "Said she had something to attend to." Susan shrugged. "She seemed a bit riled up. Which makes sense after what Gerry overheard."

"I can't believe she left," I said. Had I missed my chance?

I caught myself on a yawn and realized I'd better get on my way if I was going to spend some quality time in my own cottage, get myself some dinner and a decent sleep before my early start in the morning.

CHAPTER 16

*S*unday morning came around too quickly, and I was back in the kitchen, twisting what would become apricot Danish pastries into shape.

Gerry was happy to find me alone in the kitchen, though Pavel was due in half an hour. "I'm telling you, Pops, Sol and his missus were going at it hammer and tongs in here. He was banging the pots about and the pair of them accusing the other of doing away with Luca."

"Why would Bobbi confront her husband like that? Did she say why she thought he'd killed the deli owner?"

"No. Not that either of them was listening to the other."

"And what possible reason could she have for murdering Luca?"

"It's a puzzle," Gerry agreed.

"Sol and Bobbi were at choir practice together. There hadn't appeared to be any bad blood there. But then suddenly there was all this animosity. Where did it come from?" Had it been bubbling under the surface the whole time and I hadn't noticed? Or had something, or someone, provoked it?

Sol wasn't due in the kitchen until later, and I couldn't figure out if this was a good or bad thing. I wanted to subtly ask some probing questions, but there was also part of me that didn't want to know the answers. I'd grown fond of Sol over the past couple of weeks, and I didn't want to believe that he was capable of violence. Especially not something as conniving as murder by food poisoning. But if anyone could find the right mushrooms to kill someone, it would be Sol. He knew more about local ingredients than anyone, *and* he was part of the village foraging club. It sent a cold shiver down my spine just contemplating the idea. But what was the motive? Was Sol a jealous type? Had Luca flirted with Bobbi like he did every woman and Sol took the whole thing too seriously? Like, all the way serious?

Gerry and I couldn't discuss the strange events anymore, as Pavel arrived. "Smells good," he said, watching me put the apricots onto the pastry. I'd macerated the fruit in cardamom and sugar, and the combination really did smell delicious. At least there was one thing I was certain about: These pastries were going to make the inn's breakfast customers very, very happy.

I nestled each apricot slice inside my dough, sprinkled over some cardamom and brown sugar and sent the lot into the ovens—remembering to wish them well, of course.

I was about to begin my almond croissants when there was a knock on the swing doors.

That was strange. Pavel looked at me, so I called out, "Come in," in my most chef-sounding voice.

To my surprise, Adam Lane walked in, looking sleepy in a slightly crumpled white shirt and indigo trousers.

Pavel looked wary—a knock from the police in the early hours of Sunday morning has that effect on people.

"What are you doing here?" I asked, trying to act casual but desperate to know if there had been any new leads in Luca's death.

"Is that coffee?" he asked, looking slightly desperate. "The dining room's not open yet."

I poured him a cup and topped up my own. Pavel declined and went back to frying bacon. I leaned against the worktop. Adam Lane did the same so that we both stared at my work surface, covered in flour and drips of batter. I died a little inside. I hadn't got to the cleaning-up part of my routine yet.

"We've had some new information, and several people confirm what you told us yesterday," Adam said, "how Luca was a mushroom connoisseur if there is such a thing, and there was no way he'd mistakenly cook death caps. With their statements secured, we can officially treat the death as suspicious."

Phew. I was glad the pressure was off me to convince the police.

Adam took a long pull on his coffee. "I'm here so early as I need to talk to Florence." He took another drink of coffee.

"Florence?" I raised my brows. "Is she in trouble? For leaving the scene of the crime?" My heart began to beat double fast. Had I dropped my friend in it big-time? There was nothing more serious than being on the wrong side of a murder investigation. Running away had not been Florence's coolest move, but how much trouble could she be in?

Adam said, "Background tracing showed that Luca was originally from Genoa. I was hoping she might translate when I put a call in to..." Adam stopped talking and pulled out his iPhone. In the worst attempt at Italian pronunciation I've ever witnessed, he said, "*Commissario di Polizia* in Genoa."

"Right. I can see why you need Florence."

"Languages are really not my forte," he agreed.

"But it's a Sunday."

"Yes. The Commissario will speak to us from home."

I didn't imagine Florence wanted a man in her room this early unless she'd invited him. She'd be preparing herself for the day, so I told the detective I'd fetch her.

Adam nodded. "Tell Florence we'll release her in time to get ready for filming."

I climbed the stairs to Florence's room, wondering what kind of mood she'd be in when I knocked. I wasn't really her favorite person at the moment. But it was good that the police were investigating Luca's death more seriously. I didn't know much about Genoa in Italy. Okay, I didn't know anything. Was it by the sea? I guessed Florence would know.

I reached the door to her bedroom and got that sinking feeling I used to have as a kid before an exam or a trip to the dentist. Here I was, Poppy Wilkinson, communicator with ghosts and otherworldly spirits, afraid to knock on the door of my high-maintenance friend so early on a Sunday morning. *Get ahold of yourself, Pops.*

I braced myself and then rapped on the door with my knuckles three times. "Florence?" I whispered, mindful of the other guests sleeping soundly at 6:45 a.m. on a Sunday.

To my huge surprise, Florence opened the door after only

a few moments. She was wearing an eggplant-colored kimono, and her hair was mussed from the pillow.

"Poppy?" she said blearily, covering her mouth in a yawn. "Whatever is the matter?"

I was astounded she was awake at all, but I kept that nugget of information to myself. I explained that Sgt. Lane was downstairs in need of a translator. "It's important work," I said. "You'd be doing something immensely valuable for the investigation."

While I'd been talking, Florence had gestured for me to come into the room. I was shocked at how messy it was—the bed unmade, sheets and blankets rumpled; three bottles of water on the bedside table, each one at a different stage of being drunk; underwear and pantyhose thrown haphazardly over the damask chair, and several mugs with teabag strings hanging from their rims. But it was the lotions that really got to me. So many pots and tubes on the small coffee table and across the windowsill. Florence caught me looking and laughed.

"I'm a whirlwind when I'm stressed," she said, shrugging prettily. "It drives my poor housemates mad. Any time I'm under pressure to learn lines or lose an extra pound for a dress fitting, then I create chaos."

"But you'll come down and help, right?"

Florence said she had to get ready for filming first, but after admitting that would take well over an hour, she put on the most gorgeous pair of cashmere sweatpants I'd ever seen and a white T-shirt and pulled her long mane into a messy bun on top of her head. Florence looked beautiful even without makeup. Sometimes life just wasn't fair.

We descended the stairs together and entered the pub.

Adam had moved to the bar, talking with Eve, who'd just arrived and was getting things opened up.

"Is there coffee?" Florence asked. "If I'm to help the police solve a crime, I must have coffee."

"I'll have your espresso ready in a jiff," Eve promised.

Adam gazed at the espresso machine with the same longing as Florence. I wasn't as desperate, but I wouldn't say no to an Americano.

"You can use the office if you like," Eve said, pointing to the small room off the bar where she did the bookkeeping and other administrative tasks.

Florence turned up her beautiful nose. "Looks stuffy. Can't we sit out here? There's no one about." As I prepared to go back into the kitchen, Florence said, "No, Poppy. I want you to stay."

I was only too happy to have a chance to listen in. Having been present at Luca's end, I felt connected to him and wanted whoever caused his death to be held accountable.

Adam took Florence to a table, and she winced when he pronounced the Italian term for the superintendent of police. He'd put the phone on speaker, and we all settled at the table. Eve brought over the coffees. Florence downed her espresso in a single gulp, then asked how long it would take, obviously concerned about getting ready and heading to the tent on time for the showstopper.

"Not long." Adam was busy flipping through the pages of his notebook, found what he was looking for and hit the dial button on his smartphone. I watched Florence visibly transform. She sat a little straighter. Her expression became more concentrated, firmer. Her mood shifted from tired and irritated to professional and calm. To be honest, I was in awe.

Florence was preparing for her new role as translator in a murder investigation, and she was going to act the part, right down to the little details.

As the foreign dial tone rang, Adam looked at Florence and asked, "It's *ciao* to say hello, right?"

Florence cracked a smile. "Best to let me do the talking."

"Can you explain that it's the British police calling about a past Italian resident who has been murdered? Give him my name and tell him I'm stationed in the Somerset district. He's expecting my call. Introduce yourself as the translator."

She nodded as a gruff voice said, "*Pronto.*"

"*Buon giorno,*" Florence said. Then launched into a flood of Italian. I caught the word "*scusi*" and then Luca's name.

I was in awe of how fast her brain must be working right now.

There was a pause as the *Commissario di Polizia* replied in Italian and then Florence asked for Luca's date of birth and place of birth.

Adam gave her the details.

"The Commissario is looking for him on their system."

Florence nodded again and then burst into a rapid Italian. It was such a beautiful language, so lyrical and lilting.

"He says the name sounds familiar, but he's not sure why."

I looked at Adam in surprise. Why would the Italian police recognize that name? Was Luca a well-known criminal in Italy? Maybe that was why he'd ended up in an obscure village in Somerset. The plot was thickening.

I could tell Adam was having the same thoughts as me. He scribbled in his notebook—something illegible, much to my annoyance. Was there like a secret bad handwriting club that only the police and doctors were allowed membership to?

More chatting in Italian. I could tell Florence was getting excited. "Now he knows why he remembered that name."

My pulse quickened, and I felt my body brace for bad news. As much as Luca didn't strike me as some dark criminal mastermind, you never really knew about people's pasts.

Florence frowned. "Luca was an opera singer. Quite famous..." She glanced at us. "Though I'd never heard of him."

An opera singer? Well, that made a kind of sense. But how had Luca ended up here, running a deli, instead of touring with some renowned opera company?

I could hear the Commissario speaking super fast. Both Adam and I were watching Florence's face intently, waiting.

"His career was going well. ... He was really quite famous in Italy. ... Part of a respected company. ... Many people knew his voice. ... The Commissario and his wife are big opera fans...they go once a month to see the latest production."

That was great for the Commissario and his wife, but like, could he get to the point?

Florence's eyes widened. "Luca was embroiled in a... what's the word...a scandal!"

Adam looked up from his notebook and glanced at me. A scandal?

"What kind of scandal?" I asked.

Florence was nodding along to the Commissario's rapid voice. "My goodness," she said.

Argh, this was so frustrating. I was dying to know what had happened.

The Commissario stopped speaking, and Florence

cleared her throat. *"Grazie."* She looked at us, obviously entranced by what she'd been told. "Luca slept with the wife of the *Assessore alla culture!"*

Adam asked what that was.

"It's a political position, the cultural ambassador to the area. The politician was very well connected, you see. He knew everyone." She paused again. "He essentially black-balled Luca and made it so no one allowed him to sing with them. All theaters and opera houses blacklisted him."

Adam shook his head in amazement. "Seems he slept with the wrong man's wife," Adam said in a dry tone. "Ask the Commissario what Luca did after he'd been blackballed."

Florence rapidly translated and then repeated the Commissario's reply. "The last they heard, he flew to England and hasn't sung professionally since."

Florence ended the call and said, "Well, what a foolish man to sleep with someone who could ruin his career." She sighed. "But also romantic."

I wasn't so sure. I thought about what I kept hearing, that Luca flirted with everyone. I wondered whether he'd gone beyond flirting and once more with the wrong man's wife. "You know what they say, the leopard doesn't change its spots."

"Si," Florence said. "It's the same in Italian, *il lupo perde il pelo ma non il vizio."*

"Exactly," Adam agreed. "Whose wife was Luca carrying on with here in Broomewode, I wonder?"

I swallowed. I had an inkling but was conflicted. I didn't want to jump to conclusions, but I couldn't deny the cold facts of what Gerry had overheard and reported back to me. Despite my reservations, I knew I'd have to reveal my insider information to the police. I took a deep breath and then said I'd overheard Sol and his wife, Bobbi, in the kitchen arguing and accusing each other of murder.

Florence gasped.

Adam breathed out heavily. "You did?" he asked. "When?"

"Yesterday afternoon. But it made no sense. They'd both been at choir practice, singing songs in Luca's memory. And then they were at his wake."

"Perfect cover-up, if you ask me," Florence said.

Gaurav wandered in, fully dressed and looking for coffee. Florence gasped. "What's the time?"

Adam answered that it was half past seven, and Florence flew up. "I must get ready for filming." I reached out and grabbed her hand, remembering something else. "Before you go, remember what you told me about a woman on her way to Luca's deli holding sheets of music? And then you pointed her out to me yesterday in the pub? And I told you that it was Sol's wife? You talked about her handbag?"

But Florence slipped from my grasp. "Yes, yes, but I have to get ready. I can't be late." And with a quick air kiss, she raced upstairs. I groaned. Florence was an important witness. But obviously, her getting made up in time and ready for the cameras was more important than solving a murder. I'd tell Adam myself, and she could give a statement later. But despite feeling a little closer to the truth, my heart was heavy. Right about now, Sol, my boss and a man I liked, was looking very guilty.

CHAPTER 17

"**D**on't worry," Adam said as I mournfully watched Florence disappear. "Hembly is on his way here already. No doubt he'll want to interview Sol. Do you know what time he gets in?"

I nodded, kind of not believing that I'd managed to land my new boss in trouble with the police. I was hardly about to get employee of the month. "In half an hour," I said. "Pavel is on breakfast now, and then Sol will lead the lunch preparations."

Adam nodded. "Don't look so worried. The dispute between Sol and his wife could have been a marital spat. You don't know what's going on in their marriage."

"I can't believe Sol would hurt anyone—not even if his wife was having an affair. He's gruff and grumpy but not dangerous." But did I really know what the man was capable of?

My stomach was twisting and turning like I'd just stepped off a rollercoaster. But I didn't have time to sink into a pit of gloom. I had to head back to the kitchen. Pavel was bringing out the breakfast dishes, and I had to help and get started on the cakes for afternoon tea.

As if Pavel could read the conflicted emotions on my face when I returned to the kitchen, he flashed a small smile. "All right?"

"Yeah."

He continued scrambling more eggs. After the big personalities in the competition tent, it was nice to work with someone so unassuming. He reminded me that I couldn't ruminate. I had a job to do.

Once the pastries, croissants, and muffins were out and the dining room filling up, I stopped to wish Hamish and Maggie well today. I could see they were both looking more tense than usual. Once more, I felt relief not to be under that kind of pressure anymore.

Only the time pressure of getting all the cakes done on time.

Florence still wasn't down, so I put together a plate for her and took it up to her room.

"Oh, sweet lifesaver," she cried when she opened the door to me for the second time that morning. She was dressed in a blue summer dress, her hair perfect and her makeup nearly finished. She took the plate of food and scanned it, nodding approvingly. "And bring me another espresso, would you?"

So much for good deeds. Oh, well. Letting her treat me like the room-service waiter might soften her up so she'd answer my questions. I wasn't quite sure what exactly I suspected, yet, but I had a feeling I'd need Florence's help again.

Having delivered Florence's coffee, I headed back to the kitchen and began prep for a tropical cake. It was complicated, with many steps to follow, and I had no choice but to immerse myself in the rhythm of sifting and stirring, letting all other thoughts float away.

I would have been able to keep my focus if it hadn't been for Sol's dramatic entrance. He stomped into the kitchen, letting the door slam behind him. Not even acknowledging my presence, Sol told Pavel he'd be a bit late to help with lunch. "The bloody coppers are back and want to talk to me about Luca's death. Again. The old one said it can't wait. As if I haven't got anything better to do."

Pavel made a sympathetic noise, but I was surprised at just how gruff Sol was being. What was it with him and the Florences of this world, thinking that their work, their world, should come ahead of something as important as a murder investigation?

Sol stomped out of the kitchen as rudely as he'd stomped in, and I could hear him telling both detectives to come into his office. Hmm, where was Gerry when I needed an invisible ear closer to the action?

But I soon realized that I wouldn't need Gerry. If I moved my setup closer to the door, I could make out what the three men were saying. Lucky for me, Pavel's head was down, now engrossed in the lunch menu. I shimmied over to the other end of the steel counter and continued weighing ingredients.

As I poured out my ground almonds, adding them to the mix, Adam told Sol the police were now treating Luca's death as suspicious.

"What's that to do with me?" Sol asked, sounding testy. "Barely knew the guy."

"You and your wife were overheard having an argument

yesterday," Hembly said, giving as blunt a response as Sol. "A heated row."

"Bobbi and I fight all the time. She's got a fiery temperament, and I don't take her nonsense. So we argue and then we make up. What's that got to do with Luca?"

Hmm, Sol was being defensive right now. It really made him sound like he had something to hide. Why go into such detail about his wife's temperament?

I stood listening.

"There were accusations of murder."

At this, Sol was quiet.

Focus on your job, Pops. Don't mess up this batch.

I added almond essence, fresh vanilla pods, and then almost dropped my knife into the mix when I heard Sol yelling.

"Why would I kill that yodeling fool?"

There was a loud clatter, and Pavel yelped. I turned to see he'd dropped a colander of potatoes. I rushed over and helped him chase the rolling fellows across the floor. We picked them up in silence, both clearly eavesdropping.

"Jealousy?" Hembly asked.

I spotted another potato making its way to the pantry door and dashed after it just as Sol's voice rose another notch.

"Yeah. He got a few solos. I'm not that hard up that I'd kill over a village choir."

I grabbed the rogue potato, which clearly wasn't the only rogue around here. Why was Sol being so defensive? It made him look, well, guilty.

I returned the spud to Pavel, who thanked me quietly. We stood together in a moment of eavesdropping solidarity and heard Hembly tell Sol he shouldn't leave the village while the investigation was ongoing. In response, Sol snarled that he had a job and a mortgage. He didn't plan on going anywhere.

"One last thing," I heard Adam say. "Where can we find your wife at this hour?"

"What do you want with my wife?" Sol practically shouted.

Pavel and I exchanged another look. Sol was not taking this questioning well at all. But Hembly, who always managed to be both calm and to the point, explained that they were in the process of interviewing everyone who was in the choir or foraging group.

The office door opened, and I scurried back to my mixer and kept my head down.

Sol's angry reaction to questioning had thrown me. I'd been so convinced he was a good man, but the rude and defensive way he'd spoken to the police suggested he had something to hide. I shuddered. Please tell me that after all the drama I'd been through the last few weeks that I hadn't ended up with a murderer for a boss? But if looks could kill, then Sol had it in him to be a killer. He came back into the kitchen glowering and immediately barked at Pavel to hurry up and peel the potatoes.

"You know the ragout special needs a long time on the stove to braise," Sol shouted. "What are you waiting for?"

Luckily Sol didn't even look at me. He continued his stomping routine, taking a box of vegetables out of the pantry and throwing it down on the worktop. He was red in the face, not even pretending that he wasn't irate after talking with the police. If Sol did have something to hide, he wasn't hiding it well.

I quickly finished my cake mix and set about dividing the

batter into six tins ready to bake. But as I took my tins over to the oven, I couldn't help but glance at Sol. He was slicing mushrooms so efficiently and deftly that my mind instantly flashed back to Luca's kitchen and the pile of deadly death caps sitting beside his bubbling sauce.

My heart sank. Could Sol really have murdered Luca?

If Luca had been playing around with his wife, I suspected Sol had it in him to be violent.

I watched the blade of my electric mixer whirring around the bowl, the icing sugar and cream cheese blending together. With a dash of vanilla and some mango puree, it would be the perfect marriage of flavors. If only all marriages were such smooth sailing. I shot another look at Sol, who by now was stirring his ragout, staring into its depths, still frowning. The mushrooms were still on his chopping board, clearly destined to be added to the dish. I wanted to level with him, ask a few questions that would put my overactive mind to rest. But I also didn't want to prod the beast. Sol was definitely not in the mood for more questions. I was going to have to get creative if I wanted to do a little digging of my own.

I collected the pineapples and mangoes we'd ordered in for my tropical cake from the pantry, slowing as I passed Sol.

"I much prefer using local produce," I said—casually, I hoped. "Seems such a shame to ship in tropical fruit when we have so many cool fruits growing in England."

Sol shrugged.

I was going to have to try harder. Or, more accurately, be more on the nose.

"Susan Bentley, over at Broomewode Farm, let me pick her wild gooseberries for a competition cake. They were something else. Sweet and tart. There's something so special about cooking produce from the land around you, don't you think?"

"Yup," Sol said.

Great conversation, Sol, thanks.

Clearly, I was going to push harder still. "Susan mentioned the two of you forage together."

"That's right," he said. "There's a few of us. We share tips."

Hmm, still grumpy as a mountain goat, but at least he was giving me more than one syllable.

"Did you forage any of the veg for the ragout?"

He shook his head and said it was all from the farm nearby.

"And the mushrooms?" I gestured at the chopping board.

"Oh, the mushrooms, yes. I'm making a mushroom ragout for the dinner menu. It's mostly to cater to the foragers—the whole group is booked in for dinner. They do it once a month. Kind of a pain, to be honest. They're a fussy bunch, always asking for adjustments."

My blood went cold. Now I remembered Eve telling me that Luca was always a nuisance in the pub, asking too many questions about the dishes and driving Sol crazy. I swallowed.

"But I hope this satisfies them—I only do my special ragout when the mushrooms are right."

"What are they?" Now that I looked more closely, I saw there were several kinds of mushrooms.

Sol turned from the sauce and began to point. "Chanterelles, of course. Both the golden chanterelle and the pale. Lovely. The one with the dark cap and white flecks is called the charcoal burner. And those are summer ceps."

"Wow. So many kinds."

"Foraging is like hunting treasure. I have my own secret spots."

Lost in macabre thoughts, I did my best to smile brightly. "Luca said the Italian tomatoes were the best in the world."

Sol snorted. "He would."

"Have you ever tried them? Fresh off the vine, I mean?"

He shook his head. "Never been to Italy."

Okay, Sol hadn't, but what about his wife?

I had no choice but to resist the nagging worry in my gut —there were hungry customers to satisfy, after all, and I didn't want to mess up in my new job.

While my sponges baked, I sliced the fresh fruit, trying to let the knife slip through the sweet juicy flesh without any sinister thoughts interrupting my flow.

CHAPTER 18

wo hours had passed, and I arranged the final cakes with a flourish, spooning the sliced fruit onto the center of the cake so that it piled up delightfully like a yellow fluffy cockatoo. The last step was to press flaked coconut ribbons into the sides of the cake and then, voilà— three tropical fruit cakes finished.

I'd also managed to cook Victoria sponge, carrot cake, and coffee and walnut loaf.

With the cakes done, I dusted down my apron and slipped out of the kitchen with a short and sweet "See you in a bit." Pavel waved, and Sol grunted.

Although I didn't have any solid plans, I felt a sudden, curious urge to visit the tent and watch the baking competition for a little while. I couldn't have explained what was pulling me there—it was stronger than simple curiosity. Of course, it was a given that I wanted to know what the bakers were working on and how it was going. I could imagine the fever pitch they were reaching, probably halfway through their showstopper now, manic as they mentally calculated how many steps were left and how many minutes were on the clock. So I waved goodbye to Eve and left the inn to tread the well-worn path to the tent.

It was so nice to be outside after all those hours in the kitchen. The sun beat down on my skin, warm and penetrating, so that my muscles began to relax and I could feel my body soften. I never realized how much tension I was holding in my body until it began to shift. Before long, I spotted the usual small crowd of fans outside the tent, eagerly watching the action. I joined their ranks. A few of the locals recognized me and waved.

It was strange to be outside in the viewing area, looking in. I could see each of the bakers, all deep in concentration in their different ways. Hamish was sweating and swearing under his breath (which I knew drove Fiona, the director, to distraction), Maggie was methodical and frowning, Florence made lots of noise and generally drew attention to herself, and Gaurav spun around in his workspace, trying to get everything done in time. The cameras moved among the contestants, and Gerry was standing beside Maggie, looking more judgmental than Jonathon. No wonder my ghostly sidekick hadn't been around when I needed him to join Sol's meeting with the police. He'd been down here messing with the bakers.

As interested as I was in the competition, now that I was back on the beautiful grounds of Broomewode Hall, I couldn't help but glance toward the grand manor house. I hadn't abandoned my search for my parents, but I certainly hadn't made progress this week. Now that we were into the weekend, I could visit the old gamekeeper, Mitty, and see if there was anything he could tell me about Broomewode's past.

As I gazed, a hawk—was it my hawk?—floated over the trees to the left of the tent. I made a pact to myself to find out the address from Katie Donegal and drive over tomorrow. The hawk circled the tent and then flew in the direction of the sun, gaining height and all but disappearing from view.

Reflecting on my own reasons for coming to the village, I couldn't help but wonder why someone like Luca would do the same. Yes, he was blacklisted in his home city and country and felt the need to escape, probably to somewhere that would be a stark contrast to the life he left behind. But I couldn't quite reconcile his abrupt career change. Leaving the Italian opera scene surely didn't entail turning his back on opera completely? Why hadn't he fled to another cosmopolitan city? New York or Paris or London? Why this sleepy village in the rolling hills of Somerset with no music scene apart from the church choir? Was Luca satisfied running a small business after the prestige and glamour of his previous life? It was hard to imagine.

I was so lost in thought that I didn't notice the bakers had stopped filming for a coffee break until the viewers began to disperse and wander off to get some refreshments of their own.

Florence was waving manically. I spotted the eager look in her eyes and knew she was about to ask me for a favor.

"Pops!" she cooed, loosening the ties of her apron and rushing out of the tent. "I'm so glad you're here. It's like you read my mind."

I laughed but was a little horrified. Florence's mind was not a place I wanted to get intimately acquainted with.

She went on to tell me, in a breathy, overwrought voice, that in her haste to get to the tent on time after talking to the police this morning, she'd dropped her jar of honey en route and needed some more from Susan Bentley's farm. "It's a honey emergency, Pops. My showstopper will be more like a heartstopper without it. It's life or death."

I frowned. It seemed in bad taste to compare her baking antics with actual life and death considering what had happened in the village this weekend, but it was true to Florence's penchant for drama. I doubted there was any malice in her words, just poor taste. And taste was the name of the game here.

I realized I had some bargaining power and agreed to fetch the honey if Florence would answer a couple of questions about Luca first.

She looked at me, utterly exasperated, as if solving a man's murder was an unreasonable pursuit, but sighed and nodded for me to continue.

"Why would a disgraced Italian opera singer come to Broomewode?"

Florence shrugged. "There could be a thousand reasons." But after a beat or two had passed and she realized I wasn't going anywhere until she answered, Florence suddenly looked thoughtful.

"I know what it's like to move to a different country. I went to London for school and better work opportunities," she said. "But to move to Broomewode? He must have known someone here."

I nodded. The answer was so obvious, I'd overlooked it. "That's such good thinking." My mind worked double time. Who had caused Luca to move to Broomewode? He flirted with all the women in Broomewode, but had there been someone more special that he'd kept secret?

I thought again about that handbag Florence had recognized and that Bobbi had been carrying. She said it was from Milan. What if she'd met Luca in Italy, working or holidaying there?

"Poppy?" inquired Florence. "You've gone all...well, Poppy again."

I snapped back to attention. "How far is Milan from Genoa?"

"About two hours by car," Florence replied, looking puzzled.

Hmm. That wasn't such a great distance. Was it possible that Bobbi and Luca had met and begun an affair in Italy? And, when he lost his vocation, did he follow her to Broomewode?

"Honestly, Poppy, you ask the strangest questions, but since I've answered fairly, could you please get a move on and hustle me up some honey?"

I nodded. Florence had kept her end of the bargain; it was time to keep mine. I promised I'd be back soon.

My feet found their way on the familiar path to Susan's farm while I let my thoughts roam wildly. I needed to find out what Bobbi did for a living, whether it might have allowed her to spend time abroad. Apart from her temper and a very put-together aesthetic, I really didn't have a clue about the woman. How long had she been married to Sol? Was she from the village, or had she moved here as well? I had so many questions, but it was going to be difficult to get answers. Sol was a private man, a closed book, pretty much, and I had no reason to get in contact with Bobbi. My only hope was that

Susan might know a little more about Sol and his wife—she was in the foraging club with Sol, *and* she was in the choir with both husband and wife. Surely, she'd have some insights.

A familiar bark started up. I stopped, surprised to hear Sly's excited greeting so far from the farm. I looked around the path, and then Sly burst out of the bushes, his ball between his teeth. "Hello, my sweet boy," I cried, giving his head a hearty stroke and patting his flanks. He barked again and dropped the slobbery ball at my feet. "Where's your momma?"

Another rustle, and Susan emerged onto the path, grinning and brandishing a woven basket.

"I swear that dog can smell you a mile away," she said.

"Thanks, Susan. Are you trying to tell me something?" No doubt working in a kitchen baking for hours had made me a bit aromatic.

She burst into throaty laughter. "I don't mean literally, of course. You always smell delightful, like cakes and sugary treats. But he does have a sixth sense for when you're around."

I smiled. Team Poppy was thriving. I asked what was in the basket, and Susan beamed with pride. "I've got chanterelles, and I picked some wild sorrel. And look at those lovely Penny Buns," she said, scratching at a spot on her neck. "They're very early."

I had a sudden moment of deja vu and realized that we were standing at the exact same spot where Florence and I had bumped into Luca on Friday. I shivered, and Susan asked if I was okay.

"Still trying to piece together the puzzle of Luca's death," I confessed. "But for now, I promised Florence I'd bring back some more of your honey. She managed to smash a jar this morning."

Susan rolled her eyes. We turned toward her farm, not getting two steps until I'd removed Sly from my path by chucking his disgusting ball. As he raced after it, I tried to ease into grilling Susan about Bobbi and Sol and their marriage.

But of course, nothing in Broomewode ever really went to plan. If it did, well, then life here would be just peachy. Instead, every plan I put together was thwarted. And I wasn't even talking about my quest to find my parents. I let rip with my questions. Did Bobbi travel much? How was her marriage? What gossip had Susan heard?

"I don't know, Poppy. I barely know them. Don't forget I haven't lived in Broomewode so very long."

I probed and prodded, hoping to jog her memory—a fight overheard or a moment of tenderness observed. But no. Nothing. Susan had almost no impression of their marriage. She claimed she'd barely seen them together—even at choir practice, they stood at opposite ends of the semicircle. "And obviously, Sol doesn't talk about his marriage on foraging expeditions." She insisted the conversation was firmly rooted in extolling local produce and exchanging recipes. Any anecdotes revolved around food. I mean, I could totally understand this—I was often caught chattering about cakes and pastries rather than anything more substantial—but still, I was pretty amazed Sol had managed to keep his personal life so *personal* in such a small, gossipy village where everyone seemed to know the intimacies of each other's lives.

Clearly I wasn't going to get anywhere with Susan. I was forced to drop the subject and accompany her to collect honey for Florence. I had a bright thought and asked for a second jar for myself and a carton of happy eggs. She'd bundled the lot into the similar basket to the one she'd used to collect the mushrooms, and after checking the time with some alarm, I hurried back towards the tent, giving Sly a quick stroke goodbye, of course.

As I WALKED BACK to the tent, I couldn't help but feel frustrated at how difficult it was to get to the bottom of Broomewode's many mysteries. People here either spoke so freely it was shocking or else they were a closed book. Why was there nothing in between?

I felt stumped on all sides, no closer to understanding Luca's death and no closer to finding out about my own beginnings. I thought back to my phone call with Joanna. I'd been replaying the conversation in my mind over and over, hoping she'd have some concrete knowledge to share when I met her in person. We could have simply talked on the phone, but she'd clearly wanted to meet. Why? She was obviously a busy woman, and I was a complete stranger. Despite the warmth in her voice, there'd been something guarded about Joanna. And my sleuthing skills were all pointing towards something being off.

I was musing on this very fact when raised voices interrupted my confused thoughts.

"But I love you!" a man's voice cried.

I stopped in my tracks. Who did that voice belong to? It

was familiar, yet I couldn't quite place it. A woman sniffed in response. Was she mocking him or crying?

"Do you hear me, Vera? Why won't you say something?"

Now I recognized the voice. Vera's admirer, the lovelorn Logan.

"I love you. Why won't you marry me?"

Whoa. I'd just stumbled on a very awkward-sounding proposal. I could have answered his question: because he sounded needy and desperate.

I turned the corner and spied the two star-crossed not-lovers by a bayberry bush. Vera was battling tears, wiping her eyes with a shaking hand, while Logan looked positively desperate. This was so not what a woman dreamed of when they imagined being proposed to—not that I had any experience of being proposed to.

"Please, Logan, don't."

But Logan was not hearing Vera or reading the obvious signs. He stooped down to try to kiss her when I decided to end the awkward scene. I coughed loudly, and they both spun around.

"Hi there," I said brightly, as if oblivious to the intense proposal I'd stumbled across.

"Hi," Logan murmured, a blush rising up his neck. Vera turned away.

"I need to be..." He trailed off and pointed at something in the distance. "Off."

He turned in the direction I'd come from and scurried away. Vera glanced around to see he was gone, looking absolutely mortified.

As soon as he was out of earshot, I asked Vera if she was okay. She'd stopped crying but still looked stunned, as well she might after such a proposal. She mumbled a response I couldn't quite catch and dabbed again at her cheeks.

I was at a loss at how to comfort Vera, but I did have some questions for the tearful woman, and there was no time like the present. We headed back toward the inn and tent. Cheerfully, I said, "I wouldn't be crying if I had all the men in the village proposing to me."

Vera looked shocked. "Not all the men. Just Logan." She rolled her eyes at the name.

But I had an idea. "That wasn't your first proposal, was it?"

Again, Vera shot me that sweet Bambi look of surprise. But those wide dark eyes couldn't fool me. "Whatever do you mean?" she finally replied when it was clear that I wasn't budging.

"Luca proposed too, didn't he?"

Vera gasped and stopped walking. "How did you know?"

Phew. I'd joined the dots, and it had paid off. "Just a hunch," I said. "Why haven't you told the police?"

Vera shrugged and then looked ashamed. "I thought it would seem like I was boasting. And the poor man's dead, so I'll never marry him now."

"Were you engaged?"

"No."

"So you turned down his proposal?"

Vera began to walk again, much more slowly this time. She avoided my gaze. "Maybe turning down proposals is a running theme of mine."

I could see that Vera was deeply uncomfortable, trying to deflect my questions about Luca, but I was determined to get to the bottom of this mystery. Someone had to have some answers round here. "Why was his last message to tell you he was sorry?"

"That was only a tarot card reader. I'm sure they make things up."

Ha. If only Vera knew the depths of Eve's skills. Not simply *just* a tarot card reader, Eve was a deeply intuitive witch with powers that would blow Vera's mind. Even though I couldn't spill the beans, I wasn't going to let Vera get away with brushing Eve's words under the carpet. I was a baker. I knew how many crumbs festered in there. Instead, I pointed out how Vera had burst into tears at the message. "There had to be something real about those words for you to react that way," I said softly, realizing I was treading on pretty sensitive ground.

Vera let out a deep sigh. She raised her eyes to the sky as if Luca might be looking down on her. Finally, she said, "He had someone else."

"What?" Luca was embroiled in another romantic scandal. "But why was he proposing to you if he was with someone else?"

"I don't know." Vera's voice trembled. Oh dear. That was not what I was going for. I wanted truth, not tears.

"I think it would really help the police to find the person who'd murdered Luca if they knew more of the story."

She looked at me in alarm. "But his death was an accident. There's nothing to say otherwise. I thought the police were involved just as a precaution."

Oh, she could not be that naïve. "Do you really believe Luca would make a mistake with mushrooms? He was an expert forager."

Vera shook her head. "You're right," she whispered. There

was a pause as Vera tried to gather her thoughts. I tried to keep my cool and not put too much pressure on her, but I had some ideas and no solid answers.

"Luca asked me to marry him, but I'd seen him with another woman. And he knew I'd seen them."

"Who?" I all but yelled.

But Vera ignored me. She was lost in a painful memory. "He was trying to win me back. He said he was going to break it off with her. He promised. And I believed him." She stopped and turned to me. "And then he died."

"Who was it, Vera?" I asked again. "A broken heart or a shattered ego can be motive for murder. And what more simple murder weapon than a pile of innocuous mushrooms?"

Vera looked at me wide-eyed again. I nodded.

"But she's not a forager," Vera whispered.

"No," I agreed, my mouth set. "But her husband is."

"How did you know?"

"Just call it another hunch. The woman Luca was having an affair with was Sol's wife, Bobbi, right?"

Vera looked astounded. "Yes," she said. "It was Bobbi. I saw him with Bobbi."

CHAPTER 19

*V*era and I parted ways where the path forked. I ran to the tent to deliver Florence's honey.

I didn't know whether to be smug that my hunch had been right (with a little credit due to Gerry's excellent eavesdropping skills, of course) or saddened by another tale of romance gone wrong. Thanks to his wandering eye, Luca had lost his career, but did he learn? No. He'd messed things up with Vera because of Bobbi, who happened to be someone else's wife. It didn't make sense to me. Almost as though Luca had an inner demon making him destroy everything good in his life. His career, his love. And possibly those tendencies had led to his untimely death.

I couldn't understand where people even found the time to have affairs! With my coven, crew of familiars, and a job to hold down, finding time to search for my birth parents was a squeeze, let alone fit in a romance.

I walked double time back to the tent. Filming had already begun, and I passed the honey to one of the set runners, who promised to drop it off at Florence's workstation. I hoped I'd made it in time to be useful—otherwise I wouldn't hear the end of it. But stumbling into the middle of Vera's awkward proposal had unlocked a vital part of Luca's life story. This new information would be able to propel the police investigation forward. But the connotations of this revelation shook me to the core, and the words Bobbi and Sol flung so casually at each other yesterday deepened in significance. Had Sol found out about the affair and decided to end it permanently? The afternoon air was warm and mellow, but I shuddered, suddenly cold.

I was lost in thought before I realized someone was calling my name. Up ahead, Benedict and Edward waved at me. I walked over and then let my gait fall to the same speed as theirs.

"I'm sure Poppy can help us," Edward said. "It's about Katie Donegal."

"Is she all right?" I felt suddenly alarmed. Katie had broken her arm a couple of months ago, and I worried she might have had another accident.

"She's fine," Edward reassured me. "But her birthday's coming up. Mitty's very keen to do something for her."

Benedict said, "We usually give her a bonus so she can buy herself something, but Mitty wants a party."

"That's so sweet," I said. "And it sounds like his recovery is coming along well." The former gamekeeper had had a stroke.

"He's getting stronger every day and credits Katie Donegal with much of his recovery," Edward said.

"What can I do?" I was happy to help. I liked Katie.

Benedict said, "If we get the kitchen staff to make her a cake, it won't be a surprise."

"I'd be happy to make her a birthday cake," I said before they could ask.

Benedict looked pleased. He'd caught the sun, and his skin was a golden color, a little red around the nose. "Thank you." He smiled, and I smiled back.

"You've been at the farm?" Edward asked, pointing to the basket.

I told them both that I was initially on an errand for the ever-demanding Florence but was struck by the idea that honey and eggs would make a perfect gift for a convalescent.

Benedict raised a brow at me curiously, as if to say, *What is she on about now?*

"I'm going to visit Mitty," I explained.

"Oh, what an excellent idea," Benedict said, beaming.

I was surprised, in a pleasant way, to hear him so enthusiastic. Usually anything I said to him was met with rolled eyes or soft sighs of exasperation.

"Katie Donegal has been looking after him. I can take you to her cottage, if you like?"

Another chance to pry some Broomewode Village info out of Katie? Sign me up.

Edward excused himself to tend to some estate matters, and Benedict and I were left walking to Broomewode Hall together. The birds were singing, and after a few moments, the silence between us felt natural and easy, like we were old friends, companions even, with no need to fill the gaps between talking. For the first time all weekend, I felt relaxed.

We kept walking until I realized that Benedict had escorted me to a small single-story outbuilding not far from the Broomewode Hall kitchen. The sign read Primrose Cottage. "It's where Katie lives," he said gently, knocking on the door three times. "I'll leave you to it, but send Mitty my best. Tell him I'll be over to visit next week."

I thanked Benedict and then wasn't sure what to do. There was an awkward pause, then he rested his hand on my shoulder for a moment before squeezing it and walking away. It was a tender gesture, one that surprised me. His grip was strong, and I could still feel the impressions his fingers had made on my skin. I probably would have stayed stumped if Katie hadn't opened the door.

"Poppy!" she said. "What a pleasant surprise. Come in, come in. Don't you look bonny today. Why, your cheeks are all flushed with health."

I laughed. It was a long time since someone had actually paid my appearance a compliment. I was used to Florence telling me what was wrong the whole time, fiddling with my clothes and suggesting some alternatives. Not to mention my best friend Gina, who, with the utmost love of course, took pleasure in tweezing my eyebrows and snipping my hair until I looked more "put together"—that was how she phrased it.

"And what's that you've got there?" Katie asked, pointing at my basket. "Don't tell me you've been kind enough to whip me up one of your infamous cakes. No one ever brings me food gifts. They think all I do is cook, you see, that it would be a waste bringing me tasty morsels, but really there is nothing nicer than being cooked for at the end of a long day cooking for everyone else."

Oh, man. This was embarrassing. I felt my cheeks turning pink. "Oh, Katie, I'm sorry. It's not a cake, but I promise I will make you one soon." Hurriedly I explained it was treats for Mitty and her from Susan's farm.

To my relief, Katie looked delighted. "That's so kind," she

said, taking the basket and ushering me through to the kitchen. "That will be very nice for his breakfast tomorrow morning. He does like a cooked breakfast, fried eggs, sausage, and bacon, even though I do try to tell him to be healthier. He's an old man and set in his ways, but you'll see that for yourself in a moment. I set him up in the guest room."

Katie set the basket on the kitchen table and finally stopped talking to take a breath. I took in the room around me. I was already a sucker for a Somerset cottage, but this bungalow was a real charmer. The stone walls had been painted a beautiful washed-out ochre, the window frames a deeper mustard, the sills laden with potted herbs, the leaves tumbling toward the generous porcelain sink. One wall was lined with shelves with mismatched crockery and utensils arranged in haphazard rows. The room smelled of something sweet—treacle, perhaps, or a sponge pudding—and the whole kitchen was flooded with warm afternoon light.

"Believe it or not," Katie said, "this place was the washing house in the old days. The manor house servants would spend days in here doing the lord and lady's washing. The original drying line is still outside, though there's not much to see there apart from me drawers." She chuckled.

I imagined the poor servants back before synthetic fabrics when the washing was a massive ordeal. I was very happy to live in modern times, when I only did washing when my basket was filled to overflowing, and even then I lacked the interest to separate my colors.

Katie put the honey in a cupboard and the carton of eggs on the side. "I suppose you're not really here to listen to me natter on. Let me just see if Mitty is awake and decent enough to receive visitors."

I thanked Katie and waited with mounting anticipation. I'd been wanting to mine Mitty's local knowledge for so long, and now the moment was within reach. After a couple of minutes, Katie called out that Mitty was ready, adding a warning not to exhaust the poor man.

I followed the sound of Katie's voice, traveling down a narrow corridor painted the same warm ochre as the kitchen until I saw Katie hovering by an open door.

"Go on in, luvvie," she said in a hushed voice, "but please don't wear him out. He's still recovering and I don't want him getting upset." She touched my arm gently. "Especially if you're going to be asking about the past. Be careful of what memories you dredge up." Katie's kind eyes flashed at me. Was that a warning? Or was she simply being protective about her friend? "I'll be back in just a minute with his afternoon medicine."

I thanked Katie and walked into the room. The walls were robin's egg blue with two square windows with blue gingham curtains. An enormous cheese plant dominated one corner, and an antique-looking dresser and wardrobe filled the rest of the space. Mitty was propped up in bed reading a well-worn copy of an Agatha Christie novel. He looked up as I entered, and I couldn't believe this was the same man I'd rescued from captivity in the run-down, neglected gamekeeper's cottage. Mitty looked like a completely different man: clean, neatly cut hair, a fresh navy terry-towel robe that matched his lively blue eyes. His cheeks were clean-shaven, and he smiled at me as I entered the room. "It's Poppy, isn't it?" he said in a low, slightly trembling voice. "Please do come in. Katie-kat told me you're the lovely lady who came to my rescue. I'm afraid I don't remember anything about that day, but I'm deeply grateful." He gestured to a wicker chair beside his bed, and I took a seat.

I introduced myself properly and told Mitty how well he looked. *Compliments first, Pops, investigation second.* And after a few moments of small talk, I figured that Mitty was as trustworthy as it got and that I couldn't spin a yarn with someone who was only just recovering his memory and speech. If I was honest about my intentions, maybe he'd find it in his heart to dredge up the past and help me in my search for my mother.

I explained that I'd first come to Broomewode as part of the baking competition but that I was also searching for my mother. "She used to work at the big house, about twenty-five years or so ago." I pulled out the photo of my mother, which I'd taken to keeping in my wallet.

I passed it to Mitty, and he held it close to his face, his mottled hands shaking a little. "Valerie," he breathed.

He recognized her! This was the moment I'd been waiting for. I held my breath, silently urging him to continue.

His eyes took on a whimsical look. "Now that's a scene which takes me back. It's been many a year since they threw a garden party." I watched him study the photograph, holding back my burning questions to let Mitty's memories come flooding back. In the photograph, my mother was laughing, frozen in time by the camera, mouth open and eyes crinkled. She was tall and slight, wearing a high-waisted patterned skirt and a pink halter-neck top. In her ears hung delicate drop earrings, though I couldn't make out the stone. She *did* look a bit like me around the mouth. And maybe the eyes, too, but it was hard to tell with them so full of laughter. She was part of a laughing group of young people.

"And Valerie was your mother. Well, well."

Before I could answer, *Yes yes yes, tell me everything you know,* Katie strode into the room brandishing a bubbling glass of liquid. It was a pale gray color and not in the slightest bit appetizing. "Here you are, Mitty. Time to drink up."

But Mitty waved the glass away, still staring at the photo of the garden party. He raised his eyes and looked at me and then to Katie. "Doesn't she look like her father?"

Er, what did he just say? Father? What?

I stared at Katie, incredulous. But she avoided my gaze. "Never mind that," she said. "You get this tonic down you." She sat next to him on the bed, handing him the glass and blocking my view of his face.

Mitty took the tonic and began sipping the liquid so slowly, I felt like I was going to scream. I was bursting to ask who he thought I looked like, and what did he know of my father? But if Katie could sense my frustration, she didn't let on. Instead, she launched into an elaborate description of the honey and eggs I'd brought over from Susan's farm. Every time Mitty stopped drinking and opened his mouth to speak, she told him off in a schoolmistress tone and lifted the glass back to his lips. I wasn't being paranoid: Katie was definitely stopping Mitty from saying anything further, even going as far as to speak over him when he did manage to get a word or two out. It was infuriating!

What's more, the moment Mitty finished his medicine, it seemed as if his earlier energy had been drained from him. But Katie looked satisfied. She turned to me and explained that the medicine made him sleepy. "Maybe you could pop back another time, luvvie?"

Now it was my moment to become speechless. What was Katie doing? Why did she want to cover up what Mitty had said? She turned from me and asked Mitty if he'd like a cup of chamomile tea. But Mitty just looked at her blankly and yawned.

"What did you mean just then?" I asked Mitty quickly, "about me looking like my father? Who is it that I look like?"

But now it was my turn to be given a blank stare. Mitty shrugged and said, "I'm sorry. I can't quite... I can't..." he trailed off. "I can't seem to remember."

Katie lowered her voice. "Let's leave him to sleep, shall we? Too much talking wears the poor old soul right out." She took the photo from him and handed it back to me.

She held the door open for me and I had no choice but to leave the room. She shut the door behind her with a gentle click.

"What happened in there, Katie?" I asked. "One moment Mitty is talking to me about the past, lucid as anything, then the next he's blank. It was like someone whitewashed his mind."

"He's in and out. Sometimes sharp as a tack, and sometimes he can't even remember my name. He's getting better, though. Give it time."

Time. Huh. How about letting the man speak when he was trying?

"But he said he knew my father. And then he looked at you as though you'd known my father too."

But Katie shook her head. "Like I said, he's not himself yet. I'm so sorry you didn't get what you were after, dearie, but I must get on with the chores now. You wouldn't believe how much extra washing I have with a guest now."

And before I realized what was even happening, Katie

had hustled me out of the cottage. "Thanks again for the eggs and honey," she called out as she swung the front door shut.

You're welcome, I thought, *but maybe not as welcome as you were earlier.*

I turned away from the cottage, trying to contain my irritation.

And that's when I saw the hawk, sitting on a low branch of a whitebeam tree, staring straight at me...or so it seemed.

"Who are you?" I asked the bird.

It flapped its wings and flew off into the blue.

CHAPTER 20

Totally frustrated, I headed back to the inn. After a few moments, I realized I was stomping, stomping like a little kid. I stopped, put my hands on my hips, and looked into the sky, Mitty's words churning around in my mind. Once again, I realized that Katie knew much more than she was willing to let on. My eyes sought out the hawk, but after eyeballing me, he'd shot off as if offended by my question. But if he was my birth dad's familiar, why the cloak and dagger? My dad had already appeared to me at the magic circles—what's more, he'd actually spoken to me. True, it was mostly just warnings about fleeing Broomewode and keeping myself safe. If only I could speak to Mitty without Katie around, then maybe I could finally get to the bottom of things. I wasn't sure how much I was buying into Katie's excuse that Mitty dipped in and out of reality. He seemed perfectly lucid before he drank the medicine. Maybe there was something in that tonic that made him fuzzy.

I'd thought from the beginning that Katie knew a lot more about Valerie than she wanted me to know. And now

Mitty had acted as though she knew my father as well as my mother.

Maybe Mitty hadn't been able to tell me more, but he'd clearly identified my father in that photograph. By process of elimination, I'd find every person in that picture if it took me the rest of my life.

As I left the manicured lawns of Broomewode Hall, my mind turned back to the other secret love affairs the village seemed to attract. Ever since I'd set foot here, one doomed relationship after another had played out with the lovely rolling hills as a backdrop. And now it seemed like my birth parents were among the cohort. I'd just assumed that no one knew my father's identity, that Valerie had covered up her pregnancy or fled from her job at the old house because she had some very British sense of scandal: She was young, unmarried and so on. But Mitty's reaction, and Katie's, too, made me certain more people might know my dad. Why was it such a secret who Valerie was in love with?

The inn was up ahead, the golden brick contrasting with the vivid green of the trees. I felt overwhelmed by secrets. My own, obviously, but also Luca and his secret affair with Bobbi, Sol's wife, *and* his secret romance with Vera. My parents, keeping their relationship a secret. And my birth. Had they hoped to keep my very existence secret? By dumping me outside a bakery the minute I was born.

I shot a longing look at the car park where my trusty Renault Cleo was parked beside Eve's red bicycle, Mavis. Part of me wanted to hop inside, put foot to gas and race back home to my cottage. I missed Gateau. I'd grown used to her following me around or disappearing completely, as was her wont. There was something so reassuring about stroking her soft black fur, and I missed her sweet meows. I'd have to bring her to work with me next week. She could spend the day playing in the gardens, chasing butterflies, or snoozing in the shade of a hydrangea bush.

I was finished working for the day, so I could go home, but I wanted to see the bakers. One of them would arrive with a glum expression, having been sent home this week, and I wanted to be part of the group hugging them and telling them how amazing they were. Had I gotten the honey to Florence in time? If she'd been sent home, I was certain she'd blame me. I also had a feeling Luca's killer might reveal themselves tonight. They wouldn't intend to, but I had a few ideas.

I took a deep breath and steeled myself for what was about to come, expecting some kind of eerie showdown taking place behind the inn's heavy doors.

But as I walked into the inn, any trepidation was immediately dispelled. Even from the hallway, I could hear the pub bustling with an early Sunday evening vibe. And when I walked through the doors to the pub, I was met with a tangible atmosphere of conviviality. Booming laugher, clinking glasses, bottles popping. The weekend was still in full swing, and it looked like no one was going to be a dampener on Broomewode's fun.

I scanned the room for any sign of Sol or Bobbi or the police until my eyes landed on the baking contestants. They were back! Which meant that for one of them, this evening was their last in Broomewode.

Maggie caught my eye and waved me over. She was smiling, but there was something somber in her demeanor. Had she had a bad bake? Surely Maggie hadn't reached the end of the line? I let my eyes flicker over the group, trying to figure out who might have lost today. Would I be able to find the right words to console them? After all, I'd been in their place. I knew the strange feeling as you realized everything you'd been working towards was now gone. It was like having the rug pulled out from under your feet—so disorientating, so distressing.

I joined the group at their table. Hamish was opening a bottle of white wine as I approached and grinned. Immediately, the twinkle in his eyes told me that he'd won the show-stopper, but he didn't want to say, as it would look like insensitive boasting to the others.

I accepted the chair next to Maggie, took a breath and asked, "So how did it go?"

There was a cacophony of noise as everyone spoke at once, and I had no choice but to laugh and beg for them to speak one at a time.

"Brilliant," Hamish said.

"*Bellissima,*" Florence cried, kissing the tips of her fingers. "A success. Second place."

"Surprising," Gaurav whispered. "I burned the caramel. Third place."

Maggie said, "Not my finest hour, I'm afraid." She sighed. "But I'll have more time now for my garden and my grand-children."

I squeezed Maggie's hands tight and told her that she was one of the finest bakers I'd ever come across. I meant it, too. Maggie had always been effortless in her creations, keeping calm, staying on top of her timings. She'd never made a silly mistake like adding salt instead of sugar or forgetting how long a sponge had been in the oven. She never lost her temper or got flustered. She was all class and quiet confidence. I wondered what had gone wrong this week.

"I'm not big on puddings," she said, as if reading my mind. "It sounds silly, but dessert isn't my thing. I like proper cakes. Or bread. A lady of simple pleasures, you might say." She laughed a light, tinkling laugh. "But I've had a ball. It's been more fun than I ever could have imagined. I'm amazed I came this far. So's my husband—every Sunday he says to me, 'What, you're going back again next week?' He simply can't believe it. He'll pretend to be heartbroken when I tell him the news, but secretly he'll be pleased to have me home again."

"Och, he just misses you," Hamish said.

"He misses his Sunday roasts, more like. I've spoiled that man. He's gotten used to Sunday dinners, slices of rare roast beef, roast potatoes, cauliflower cheese, honey-glazed carrots, and a Yorkshire pudding. Why, the man's lost ten pounds since I've been on the competition."

I looked at Maggie in earnest. She really was taking it very well. Did she feel the same strange relief I did last week? The satisfaction of knowing you've tried your very best and couldn't have done more? I'd worn myself out trying to keep up with the tough competition, pushing myself to limits I didn't even know I'd had. Maggie was probably tired of the grinding pace every weekend.

I could tell her how much she was going to enjoy not waking up in the middle of the night worrying about recipes or practicing the same bake over and over. But Maggie didn't appear to need any words of wisdom from me. She barely seemed upset and was already schooling Gaurav on the best friand recipe she'd ever made. I took the opportunity to congratulate Hamish on his showstopping win.

"I really pulled it out of the bag at the last minute," he said. "But as interesting as my baking life is, I can't help but keep my police officer cap on. Have you solved Luca's murder yet? The police have been suspiciously absent from the village this afternoon."

I frowned. Surely Vera had kept to her word? She'd promised to tell the police about Luca and Bobbi. Perhaps they were biding their time? Or could they have been called away to another case? I admitted to Hamish that the murder wasn't solved, but I had my suspicions. It was time to throw my evidence to the team and see what they thought.

I began by sharing what Florence had discovered about Luca's glittering opera career in Italy, allowing her to butt in and add her two cents. Then I explained what I'd learned from Vera (asking for a sworn oath to secrecy before it came out for real) that Luca was having an affair with Sol's wife, Bobbi, but had also asked Vera to marry him. She had wanted to say yes, claiming that Luca was the perfect gentleman.

"But that doesn't make sense," Gaurav said. "He lost a promising opera career because of an affair with a married woman. He came here and was having an affair with Sol's wife, and yet the sweet girl in the choir says he was a perfect gentleman. He even proposed. Why would he do that while sleeping with another man's wife?"

Florence threw up her hands and huffed. "Naturally, it makes sense. He's a typical, traditional man. He would sleep with a married woman but not the woman he was planning to marry. Very old-fashioned."

After her little outburst about men, Florence calmed down and said she was ravenous. I laughed—Florence's mind was either on men or food. Personally, I'd much rather stick to the food side of things. I felt strange joining them for dinner, but again, they all insisted, and since it was Maggie's last day, I didn't want to refuse. Besides, if Vera had been true to her word, then I imagined the police had already pieced together the puzzle and were on their way to the inn already.

I ordered tonight's fish special and stuck to drinking water. I had the feeling that this was the calm before the storm, and I wanted to keep a clear head if my instincts turned out to be true.

The group chattered around me, and I tried to join in their playful conversation, but my heart felt heavy. I was thinking about betrayal, between friends as well as lovers. Betrayal that had turned deadly.

$\mathcal{I}$ kept my eye on the long table with the sign on it saying it was reserved. This was the table set aside for the foragers' dinner. As they arrived, they all went to the bar for a drink before sitting down to dinner. I spotted Sol's brother immediately. In a white T-shirt, he sported a full sleeve of intricate tattoos on hefty arms like his brother. He was smiling and joking with another man I didn't recognize. Then there was Lauren, talking to the young chef at Broomewode Hall, both of them looking lovely with swinging, iron-straight hair, and to my surprise, there was Lovestruck Logan, looking unhappy. No wonder, the way his proposal had gone. Susan and Reg arrived and joined in.

I watched the group interact at the bar, saw how familiar and easy they were with each other. But it occurred to me that no one seemed to be in mourning for Luca. No tears, no quiet looks or huddled conversation—they were in full weekend mode. Only Susan and Vera had openly appeared to be upset by Luca's death. Had the singer-cum-deli owner really kept himself so separate from people in the village that they didn't know him well enough to truly mourn his passing? The thought was too sad to contemplate. I was still amazed that a man so full of life and verve, who'd had a budding opera career, could come to England disgraced and all but hide away. Had Luca really been content to simply sing in the local choir? Hadn't he missed the glamour and glitz of the Italian theater circuit? Of hearing his voice soar across sold-out theaters? The only thing about his past life that Luca had retained was the chronic flirting, which had thrown him yet again into hot water. The hottest water ever. I shivered again as my mind flashed back to that bubbling pan of mushrooms.

Philly and Eve brought out our food. We were a small group but a chatty one. Even Maggie soon perked up when her shepherd's pie was in front of her.

Despite his winner's high, I noticed that Hamish was picking at his food, his gaze traveling back to the bar, where the foragers were enjoying a cocktail ahead of dinner. I wondered what was going on inside that head of his—was he starting to connect the same dots as me? I was about to ask exactly that when DI Hembly and Adam Lane walked into the pub. Behind them was Bobbi.

"She's been crying," Hamish said to me quietly. "Look at her eyes. Red and puffy."

"And her hair is totally ruffled," I added, "as if she's been running her hands through it continuously. She was so carefully put together yesterday—not a single blond strand out of place."

"See her shirt?"

I nodded. Bobbi was wearing a long-sleeved linen shirt

over loose cotton trousers and a red tank top. The sleeves were rolled, but still it hung on her.

"It's not hers. Someone has given her that to keep warm or to feel comforted."

Hamish was so smart. Squinting, I realized I recognized that shirt. "No way," I murmured aloud.

Hamish asked me what was wrong.

"Unless my mind is playing tricks on me, that's Luca's shirt. I swear he was wearing that on Friday when Florence and I bumped into him foraging."

"You don't say."

We both watched as Bobbi said goodbye to the detectives and joined Susan Bentley at the bar. Susan put an arm around her instantly, secure in her role as comforter. But I felt protective about Susan. She was always the first to show compassion, but Bobbi wasn't exactly a prime candidate for sympathy—she'd been cheating on her husband, after all. Susan would have told me off for being judgmental if she'd known what I was thinking, but my train of thought was interrupted by the detectives heading straight for our table.

"Miss Cinelli?" DI Hembly said. "May we have a word?"

Florence went white. She cast a look in my direction, but I had even less of a clue why they wanted to talk to Florence again. I shrugged ever so slightly, hoping she'd understand this had nothing to do with me whatsoever.

Although Florence was clearly shaken, she leapt into actress mode, and there was a perceptible shift in her body and expression. She flashed a winning smile at both detectives—especially at Adam. "How can I help?" she said sweetly.

"You were seen coming out of Luca's house the day of the murder."

Florence spun in her chair and looked at me as if to say, *How could you?* But I hadn't! Yes, I'd told the police Florence was with me the night Luca was murdered, but I'd never revealed she'd been there earlier in the day. I'd kept that little nugget of information to myself—not that I could say that out loud right now. I hardly wanted to draw attention to that fact in front of the detectives. Instead, I tried to communicate only using my eyes. I probably looked like I was having a mild aneurism, but Florence must have caught on, because she began to look around the bar wildly.

"Aha!" she cried, pointing at the bar. I followed her elegant, wagging finger. It had landed on Bobbi. "You! You went to see Luca after I did."

Florence stood up so suddenly that her chair clattered back onto the stone floor. The entire pub fell silent, and all turned to look at our table. Her pointing finger swept across the air. "What's your game? Yes, you with the knockoff hand-bag. You went into the deli after I did, and Luca was very much alive when I left."

There was a collective gasp. Florence was practically bristling with indignation, but there was also something electric about her, glimmering and alive. My goodness, did that girl thrive on attention.

I watched with horror as Sol emerged from the kitchen. All the yelling must have filtered through, and now he stared at his wife with the most intense loathing I'd ever seen. He was holding a basket of sliced baguette, which I assumed was meant to accompany the wild mushroom ragout.

But if Bobbi had seen her husband, she didn't show it.

Instead, tears tracked down her cheeks, and she struggled to form her words. "You could have returned after I left. I didn't kill him. I wouldn't... I loved him."

"Ha!" Florence looked at her with contempt and pity. "But you could never have him, could you? He saw you as a plaything, nothing more." She shrugged her shoulders as if to suggest Bobbi was a speck of dirt to be shimmied off.

Bobbi gulped. "How do you know?"

"I'm Italian, darling. I know how Italian men work."

I watched Bobbi visibly shrink. I knew that feeling—when you'd been caught out and wished you were invisible. I'd experienced it just last week when my breadmaking skills were put to the test and I'd embarrassed myself on national TV.

With a loud clatter, Sol put down the bread. But if Florence noticed, it certainly didn't slow her down. She was on a roll now, her cheeks flushing, her eyeballs widening to show the whites.

"And that's why you killed him, isn't it? Because he was planning to marry *her!*"

I followed Florence's gaze and realized that Florence was gesturing at Vera. She was tucked in a corner, and as the whole pub turned to stare, she buried her face behind her hands.

"No!" Bobbi cried. "That's not true!"

"Vera was Luca's one true love. She was the woman he wanted to marry. And you couldn't stand it," Florence said, gaining momentum now. So much for keeping quiet about what I'd told her in confidence. And yet, she was shaking things loose. Her voice was loud and strong, with no hint of nerves or uncertainty. As bad as it was that Florence was clearly enjoying this, she was doing a superb job of leading the showdown. But if my instincts were right, then she was getting a little ahead of herself.

Bobbi was crying louder now. She insisted she didn't kill Luca. She wouldn't. And then a change came over Bobbi, and I could see that she was beginning to tire of being embarrassed and ashamed. The color returned to her face, and she wiped the tears from her cheeks, dabbing beneath her heavily made-up eyes to wipe away the murky black smudges. Next, she swiveled on her stool and pointed again at Vera, who was watching the scene in front of her with horror. "I saw you making out with Luca," she said. "In the street, so brazenly, as if you had nothing to hide."

"I *did* have nothing to hide," Vera replied.

But Bobbi continued as if she hadn't heard. "He broke up with me because of you, but that wasn't enough. Your jealousy took over. You killed him."

Vera looked stunned as Bobbi berated her, trying to make out that she was crazy and possessive. That she'd punished Luca for his dalliance with Bobbi. Vera receded even farther into her corner, pale and terrified at the vitriol that flew across the room. It seemed as if it wouldn't stop, and I could see that Sol was about to intervene when Logan jumped up from the forager's table.

"Stop it!" he yelled. "Just stop it! Vera couldn't have killed Luca. She was with me that night."

For the second time that evening, the whole pub gasped. The inn's guests had gotten a special tonight—dinner *and* a soap opera.

Bobbi looked as though she couldn't believe it. "You betrayed Luca with this—this nincompoop?"

"It's true. Logan was with me Friday evening. He only came to comfort me." She stared at Logan and said very clearly, "As a friend."

It was time for me to help put an end to all this. I stood up. "But—"

Bobbi looked at me, the disgust at my intervention clear for all to see. I wasn't going to let that stop the truth. "But Logan didn't arrive at your house, Vera, until after he'd already visited Luca, isn't that right?" I turned to Logan, ready to lay out all that I had gathered from investigating this sorry case.

"You knew that Vera and Luca were in love. You knew that Luca wanted to marry Vera, but she refused, because she'd seen him with another man's wife."

Now it was Logan's turn to become pale. "What are you on about?" he said, his voice as cold as hell frozen over.

"And it was the last straw. You hated Luca. He got all the solos in the choir, and he had the woman you wanted. I saw the way you reacted in church when you were assigned one of his solos. You could barely contain your glee. It all worked out perfectly for you—with Luca out of the way, you could take his solos, and you hoped to take Vera, too, didn't you?"

Logan was shaking his head, but I could see that all the fight had been drained out of him. "If Luca had treated Vera right, well, I would have bowed out straight away. But he didn't. He cheated on her. How could anyone do that to an angel?"

Out of the corner of my eye, I saw DI Hembly remove handcuffs from where they hung, ready for action, on a loop of his belt.

"I couldn't stand to see my sweet, darling Vera be treated that way. It couldn't go unpunished."

"So you took care of it yourself."

"The best way I knew how. Use his love of foraging against him."

"How did you do it?" I asked, knowing the more he confessed, the easier the police's job would be.

"It was simple enough. I knew he'd been foraging so he'd be cooking that night. I sliced up some death caps and dropped in on him, asking some questions about foraging. He offered me a glass of wine, and when his back was turned, I dropped the chopped death caps into his *famous*"—he stopped to air-quote the word *famous*—"pasta sauce. Of course, the man couldn't stop himself from tasting his sauce as it was cooking. I waited until he was on the floor and then placed the pre-sliced mushrooms on his chopping board. I washed my glass and put it away and left." He glared at me. "I should have got away with it."

I recalled the wineglass, placed back on the shelf the wrong way up. "You were sloppy, Logan. You didn't dry the wineglass completely, and you put it back stem up. Luca's other glasses were stem down. Besides, anyone close to Luca would know that he wouldn't make a mistake like that with mushrooms."

Logan snorted. "Always thinking he knew better than everyone else, that because he was Italian, he knew everything about music and food and about love. Don't get me started on the way he treated women. Killing that man was the best decision I ever made. I did the world a favor."

"That's enough!" Vera cried, suddenly leaping to her feet.

"You didn't do the world a favor. Or me. You took the man I loved, and I hate you for what you did."

Whoa. Go Vera. She'd finally found her voice, and it belonged to a straight-talking no-nonsense woman.

DI Hembly stepped forward. "Logan Peters, I am arresting you on suspicion of the murder of Luca Romano. You do not have to say anything, but it may harm your defense if you do not mention when questioned something you later rely on in court. Anything you do say may be given in evidence."

Logan bowed his head, and the whole pub watched as Luca's killer was led away by the police.

CHAPTER 22

With Logan cuffed and taken away by the police, the pub slowly swung back to its previous buoyant mood. There was huge relief that a murderer had been caught. But there was one person who looked like she'd never be the same again: Vera. Susan was by her side, of course, and Eve had come out from behind the bar to help provide whatever comfort she could. My heart truly went out to Vera. I knew she must be blaming herself right now—if it wasn't for Logan's infatuation and his terrific jealous streak, then maybe Luca might be alive, enjoying a glass of red along with the other customers. But it wasn't Vera's fault—as I was sure Susan and Eve were already saying.

Luca had been reckless with people's hearts and landed himself in trouble often during his life. And his parting words on this earth were to tell Vera he was sorry. It was his love for her that had filled his soul before he crossed over to the other side. He was sorry for messing things up, for taking the wrong path. And, at the last, he'd understood it was Vera who mattered to him most.

The evening's drama wasn't quite over, however. I went up to the bar and asked Philly to make me a coffee. While I waited, Bobbi came out of the door to the kitchen looking shell-shocked. She came toward me. "I hope you're pleased with yourself. Now Sol's gone and chucked me out."

How was this my fault? "I'm sorry," I said, even though I wasn't really.

She sighed and settled onto a stool, fondling that Dionigi bag as though it were a beloved pet. "I suppose it was my own fault. But Luca made me feel alive again."

"You met him in Genoa?"

She blinked at me and nodded. "I didn't only meet him, I fell under his spell. He was singing in *Tosca* at the Teatro Carlo Felice." She sighed. "I didn't even know I liked opera, but my friend did, and she got us invited to a reception after the performance. Luca was charming, spoke perfect English and made me feel like I was the most fascinating woman in the world." She smiled wryly. "He was good at that. Well, one thing led to another. We fell in love, or at least I did. I thought it was mutual. A whirlwind romance. He wined and dined me; he bought me this bag." She glared in Florence's direction. "And it is not a fake."

"That must have been so exciting."

"Oh, it was. Sol is, well, you know. He's not a man to sweep a woman off her feet. I went back to Genoa a couple of times, and it was always magical. The last time Luca told me he had to be with me. He was giving up opera to come to Broomewode. I was thrilled and scared. But he promised he wouldn't interfere with my marriage." Suddenly, she scowled.

"And he never did. Even when I told him I wanted to leave Sol and be with him, he refused. Said it was the Catholic guilt, but now I know he had that vapid virgin in his sights."

"Still, he moved to Broomewode for you." And to get away from a furious husband who'd destroyed his career.

"I didn't think he'd stay, but I think he grew to love it here. He enjoyed sharing the delicacies of Italy with our village, and he liked the foraging, and of course he was the star of our little choir." She patted her bag again. "If only he'd left Vera alone, he'd still be alive. It's a judgment on him."

I couldn't agree with her, so I kept my mouth shut.

"Well, I'd better go, I suppose. I'll have to find somewhere to stay until I sort myself out."

"Maybe Sol will change his mind," I said.

She made a rude noise. "I won't. No, it's bye-bye Broomewode for me. There's a whole world out there, Poppy. I plan to enjoy it."

ONCE SHE'D LEFT, the foragers settled down to their dinner. Sol didn't sit with them, which was probably just as well. Eve quietly removed the chair and place setting that would have been Logan's.

Once our dinner was finished, Maggie told the group it was time to say a final goodbye. Strangely, I felt more upset than I did last week, when it was me being booted off the show. Maggie was perhaps the sweetest baker of them all. She was kind, caring, and so positive, it was hard to imagine the group dynamics without her. But Maggie didn't appear to be as upset as we all were as she thanked us for our support and friendship over the weeks. "I'm proud to have been part of such a lovely group," she said, kissing each one of us on the cheek.

"Keep in touch," Hamish urged. "Get the grandkids to set up your emails on your phone."

Gaurav smiled shyly and said he'd already done that for Maggie and added her on the group mailing list.

Everyone smiled. Gaurav had the most generous heart.

There was nothing for it now but to say our last goodbye and wish Maggie well on her journey.

I squeezed Maggie tight, sad to see her go. "I'll be up to visit you as soon as I can," I said. "You know I can't resist one of your scones." I detached myself from the embrace and lowered my voice to a whisper. "They really are the best in Broomewode, but promise not to tell anyone I said that. People around here are very protective about their scone recipe. I mean, it's scary."

"I promise," Maggie said warmly.

I let the others take their turn. Each of them seemed to want to say something important to Maggie. She really had touched everyone deeply.

While Gaurav and Hamish chatted with Maggie, Florence turned to me and said what a wild weekend we'd had. I agreed. Meeting Luca, our ill-fated dinner, his murder—well, it was enough to throw off even the best-laid plans. I was amazed all that drama hadn't put Florence off her baking game. But no, she looked fresh as a daisy.

"What are your plans, Pops," she said, "while we poor three spend the week in a fit of nerves and baking practice?"

Hmm. Poor three? Hardly! They were about to enter the semifinal after hundreds of contestants had applied and auditioned, twelve had been selected, and now Hamish, Gaurav, and Florence were the last bakers standing. They were lucky souls indeed.

I gave Florence my best *woe is me* expression, and she laughed.

It was moments like these that I really wished I could tell Florence the truth about being a witch. But instead, I'd have to get creative or vague. "Just catching up on some projects," I replied noncommittally. But Florence's attention had already drifted, and she excused herself to go and talk to Donald Friesen, the series producer, who'd just walked in the pub with Fiona, the director, Jilly and Arty, and Elspeth and Jonathon.

At the sight of Elspeth, my heart soared. I'd missed her so much this weekend and was desperate to tell her about all that happened. And my real plans for the coming week. My main project was to find out more about my parents, specifically my mom, Valerie. I'd have to find a way to get to Mitty when he was more alert and without Katie Donegal interfering. It wasn't the first time Katie had gotten in the way of me and information about my birth parents. I didn't understand why she was blocking my progress. It was like she had some personal investment in being a pain in my butt.

But at least Mitty wasn't my only lead. I had a meeting with Joanna to look forward to next week. I was closer to getting to the truth about Valerie and my father. I could feel it in my bones.

Thank you for reading *A Cream of Passion*. I hope you enjoyed it. Poppy's adventures in competition baking, and murder, continue in *Cakes and Pains*. Read a sneak peek below…

∽

Cakes and Pains, Chapter 1

TO SAY I was excited about meeting a woman named Joanna for coffee would be an understatement. I was so nervous and thrilled I could barely eat—definitely strange behavior for me. I baked for fun and for my living and I definitely enjoyed the fruits of my labors.

Joanna had been a school friend of a woman named Valerie who I was convinced was my birth mother. I'd had visions of my mom, mostly misty ones as I was a water witch, but I was certain it was my mother communicating with me. Unfortunately, most of our communication had been her warning me to leave Broomewode in Somerset where I had been a contestant on The Great British Baking Contest. Yes, had been. I'd made it respectably far, but bread week did me in. Luckily, the very week I was cut from the contest, I got an offer to become the baker at Broomewode Inn, so, while I was no longer in the running for the country's best baker, I could still see the remaining contestants who'd become my friends and try and discover where I'd come from.

I'd had a happy childhood with my adopted family, but I still yearned to know more about the woman who'd left me in an apple box outside a bakery while I was only a few hours old. The only clue to my identity had led me here and I felt I was close to finding out where I'd come from. I hoped Joanna might be able to help me. I sensed that my birth father was dead, but that my mother was alive. Maybe it was a foolish hope since she'd never tried to contact me and I'd never been able to find her, but I longed to know more about where I'd come from and why a young woman had done such a desperate thing as to abandon her newborn child. I sensed deep love in the visions I'd had of both my birth parents, and also fear for me.

Why? Who would want to harm me? I was a twenty-five-year old graphic artist and baker. Not exactly dangerous professions. However, no one could deny that strange and sometimes deadly things happened at Broomewode, especially when I was around.

But I felt fairly safe having coffee with an old school friend of my mother's. What possible danger could there be in a coffee date?

~

Order your copy today! *Cakes and Pains* is Book 8 in The Great Witches Baking Show series.

A Note from Nancy

Dear Reader,

Thank you for reading *The Great Witches Baking Show* series. I am so grateful for all the enthusiasm this series has received. If you enjoyed Poppy's adventures, you're sure to enjoy the *Village Flower Shop,* the *Vampire Knitting Club,* and the *Vampire Book Club* series.

I hope you'll consider leaving a review and please tell your friends who like cozy mysteries and culinary adventures.

Review on Amazon, Goodreads or BookBub. It makes such a difference.

Join my newsletter for a free prequel, *Tangles and Treasons,* the exciting tale of how the gorgeous Rafe Crosyer was turned into a vampire.

I hope to see you in my private Facebook Group. It's a lot of fun. www.facebook.com/groups/NancyWarrenKnitwits

Turn the page for Poppy's recipe for Blueberry Buttermilk Muffins.

Until next time,
Happy Reading,
Nancy

POPPY'S RECIPE FOR BLUEBERRY BUTTERMILK MUFFINS

You didn't think I was going to skip over giving you a lovely recipe, did you? Just because I'm no longer in the running for Star Baker, or even Winner of The Great British Baking Contest, doesn't mean I don't know a trick or two about delicious cakes and muffins.

Ingredients:

- 2 cups blueberries (fresh or frozen)
- 2 cups flour
- I cup sugar
- 2 1/2 teaspoons baking powder
- 1/2 teaspoon salt
- 2 large eggs (happy ones, of course, room temperature)
- 1/2 cup buttermilk
- 1/3 cup vegetable oil
- I 1/2 teaspoons vanilla
- turbinado sugar (for dusting)

Metric:

- 340 grams blueberries (fresh or frozen)
- 250 grams flour
- 200 grams sugar
- 2 1/2 teaspoons baking powder
- 1/2 teaspoon salt
- 2 large eggs (happy ones, of course, room temperature)
- 118 milliliters buttermilk (can replace with whole milk, a teaspoon of lemon juice and let stand for half an hour)
- 79 milliliters vegetable oil
- 1 1/2 teaspoons vanilla
- turbinado sugar (for dusting)

Method:

1. Preheat oven to 400 degrees (180 centigrade).
2. Sift together flour, sugar, baking powder, and salt. In another mixing bowl, whisk together eggs, buttermilk, vegetable oil, and vanilla. Pour wet ingredients into dry and mix. Then add blueberries, folding in carefully. Don't want to smash the berries!
3. Spray non-stick cooking spray into prepared muffin tins, or use liners. Sprinkle coarse sugar on top.
4. Bake 20 to 25 minutes.

These muffins make a wonderful addition to a breakfast buffet, or serve warm with butter and a touch of local honey.

Bon appétit!

Village Flower Shop: Paranormal Cozy Mystery

Peony Dreadful - Book 1

Karma Camellia - Book 2

Highway to Hellebore - Book 3

Vampire Knitting Club: Paranormal Cozy Mystery

Tangles and Treasons - a free prequel for Nancy's newsletter subscribers

The Vampire Knitting Club - Book 1

Stitches and Witches - Book 2

Crochet and Cauldrons - Book 3

Stockings and Spells - Book 4

Purls and Potions - Book 5

Fair Isle and Fortunes - Book 6

Lace and Lies - Book 7

Bobbles and Broomsticks - Book 8

Popcorn and Poltergeists - Book 9

Garters and Gargoyles - Book 10

Diamonds and Daggers - Book 11

Herringbones and Hexes - Book 12

Ribbing and Runes - Book 13

Mosaics and Magic - Book 14

Cat's Paws and Curses - A Holiday Whodunnit

Vampire Knitting Club Boxed Set: Books 1-3

Vampire Knitting Club Boxed Set: Books 4-6

Vampire Knitting Club Boxed Set: Books 7-9

Vampire Knitting Club Boxed Set: Books 10-12

Vampire Book Club: A Paranormal Women's Fiction Cozy Mystery

Crossing the Lines - Prequel

The Vampire Book Club - Book 1

Chapter and Curse - Book 2

A Spelling Mistake - Book 3

A Poisonous Review - Book 4

Abigail Dixon: A 1920s Cozy Historical Mystery

In 1920s Paris everything is très chic, except murder.

Death of a Flapper - Book 1

Toni Diamond Mysteries

Toni is a successful saleswoman for Lady Bianca Cosmetics in this series of humorous cozy mysteries.

Frosted Shadow - Book 1

Ultimate Concealer - Book 2

Midnight Shimmer - Book 3

A Diamond Choker For Christmas - A Holiday Whodunnit

Toni Diamond Mysteries Boxed Set: Books 1-4

The Almost Wives Club: Contemporary Romantic Comedy

An enchanted wedding dress is a matchmaker in this series of romantic comedies where five runaway brides find out who the best men really are!

The Almost Wives Club: Kate - Book 1

Secondhand Bride - Book 2

Bridesmaid for Hire - Book 3

The Wedding Flight - Book 4

If the Dress Fits - Book 5

The Almost Wives Club Boxed Set: Books 1-5

Take a Chance: Contemporary Romance

Meet the Chance family, a cobbled together family of eleven kids who are all grown up and finding their ways in life and love.

Chance Encounter - Prequel

Kiss a Girl in the Rain - Book 1

Iris in Bloom - Book 2

Blueprint for a Kiss - Book 3

Every Rose - Book 4

Love to Go - Book 5

The Sheriff's Sweet Surrender - Book 6

The Daisy Game - Book 7

Take a Chance Boxed Set: Prequel and Books 1-3

For a complete list of books, check out Nancy's website at NancyWarrenAuthor.com

ABOUT THE AUTHOR

Nancy Warren is the USA Today Bestselling author of more than 100 novels. She's originally from Vancouver, Canada, though she tends to wander and has lived in England, Italy and California at various times. While living in Oxford she dreamed up The Vampire Knitting Club. Favorite moments include being the answer to a crossword puzzle clue in Canada's National Post newspaper, being featured on the front page of the New York Times when her book Speed Dating launched Harlequin's NASCAR series, and being nominated three times for Romance Writers of America's RITA award. She has an MA in Creative Writing from Bath Spa University. She's an avid hiker, loves chocolate and most of all, loves to hear from readers!

The best way to stay in touch is to sign up for Nancy's newsletter at NancyWarrenAuthor.com or www.facebook.com/groups/NancyWarrenKnitwits

To learn more about Nancy and her books
NancyWarrenAuthor.com

facebook.com/AuthorNancyWarren

twitter.com/nancywarren1

instagram.com/nancywarrenauthor

amazon.com/Nancy-Warren/e/B001H6NM5Q

goodreads.com/nancywarren

bookbub.com/authors/nancy-warren

Made in the USA
Middletown, DE
09 July 2023

34772423R00119